Suddenly a Father
Hometown Hearts

Holly Jacobs

Suddenly a Father

Ilex Books
ISBN: 978-1-948311-07-6
Copyright © 2020 by Holly Fuhrmann

Previously Published as:
A Father's Name
ISBN #9780373717330
Copyright © 2011 by Holly Fuhrmann

Reviews:

"Real sparks fly between Angelina and Tyler, both very well-developed characters. Angelina's determination to do right by her son rings true, as does Tyler's willingness to help a friend in spite of the personal cost to himself." **—RT BOOKreviews**

"Award winning author Holly Jacobs writes heart warming family romances that touches her readers every time. Her latest captivating book reacquaints us with familiar character Tucker and introduces us to Tyler, an honorable man that goes above and beyond to protect his friend's reputation." **—CataRomance**

Dear Reader,

The greatest tool a writer has is the question, *what if?* I introduced this book's heroine, Tucker, in *Crib Notes,* and she's been in other stories since. In that first book, she and her friend Eli were commiserating about their problems with men and Tucker complained that she was being actively pursued by a designer suit-wearing businessman who she felt she had nothing in common with. So, I asked, what if this man, Tyler, lost everything? His job, his money, his designer suits...and most important, his good name. And what if he finds himself back in Tucker's life? That's how the idea for *Suddenly a Father* was born.

But this was a book that required a bit more assistance than usual. You see, I know nothing about cars, other than how to turn one on and how to fill it with gas, and Tucker works at a garage. And my hero lost everything because of a legal jam. The jam itself wasn't hard for me to come up with, but getting him out of his legal problems took a bit more help, which is why I spent a lovely afternoon in Erie eating lunch on the bay with a judge and an assistant district attorney. With their help, we came up with a resolution that is within the realms of legal possibility, if not probability. That is one of the best things about being a writer. I get to learn a little about a lot of things, and I also get to meet and spend time with some awesome experts from various fields.

Tucker and Tyler discover that it's not only authors who need help...everyone does. It takes a village to raise a child and to write a book, and sometimes it takes help from friends and even judges and A.D.A.s to fall in love! I hope you enjoy their story and the rest of my *Hometown Hearts* series!

Holly Jacobs

Hometown Hearts
1. Crib Notes
2. A Special Kind of Different
3. Homecoming
4. Suddenly a Father
A Hometown Hearts Wedding
5. Something Borrowed
6. Something Blue
7. Something Perfect

Suddenly a Father
Hometown Hearts

Holly Jacobs

Dedication:

They say it takes a village to raise a child...
sometimes it takes a village to write a book.
This one required a lot of outside help.

Thanks to John and Joe for the car help!

Thanks to Judge Stephanie Domitrovich and
A.D.A. Nathaniel Strasser for the legal
expertise—any legal stretches are all mine!

Thanks to Jess, Kate and Abbey, who gave me
insight into how torturous pedicures can be, and
to Jeremy Bettis Levitt, who helped me
remember what life with a one-year-old is like!

And finally, thank you to all my online friends
who helped me out with T-shirt ideas.

PROLOGUE

"HOW DO YOU PLEAD?"

Tyler Martinez didn't look at the judge; instead he glanced back at the spectators. Mellie was there, though she should have been home in bed. Her face was drawn and pale. She wore a white scarf that he'd brought home as a gift from his trip to Cannes a few months ago.

He wasn't sure why he'd noticed that, but he did. When he'd made that trip, he never realized how his life was about to change. Only a few months had gone by, but it felt like a lifetime.

The only constant in life was change.

He wasn't sure where he'd read that, or why he'd thought of it other than the truth of the statement was staring him in the face. Maybe for some people change was a good thing, but not for Tyler—and certainly not these kinds of changes.

Jason was sitting next to Mellie, anguish etched on his face. Tyler smiled in a useless attempt to reassure his best friend. He wanted Jason to believe that everything would be all right.

Mellie took Jason's hand and held it. Both Tyler and Jason knew that nothing would be all right again.

Tyler wished there was more he could do, but there wasn't.

There wasn't anything more anyone could do.

So this gesture would have to be enough.

"I don't contest the charges, Your Honor."

Tyler Martinez listened as the judge sentenced him. He watched his friends as he was led from the courtroom, knowing that when he got out of jail in six months there was a very good chance that Mellie wouldn't be waiting with Jason.

CHAPTER ONE

GARY JOHNSON'S PHONE number flashed as a missed call on Angelina Tucker's cellphone and she tried to tamp down her annoyance.

Tucker didn't date often, but when she did, she practiced a catch-and-release program. Unfortunately, Gary Johnson didn't want to be released and had been calling for days asking for another date.

She'd tried being polite, then tried to joke and pretend she was one of the guys with her let's-be-buddies pitch. Neither worked. Gary obviously wasn't getting her not-so subtle hints. She'd have to try something more direct.

The man was so dense it was going to have to be something big. Something like a swift kick or else a restraining order.

Gary's number on her caller ID had left a sour taste to what was normally her happy Monday mood. She stomped into the garage, not wanting to think about returning that phone call.

"Hey, Lou," she called by way of a greeting as she made a beeline for the coffee machine.

"What's on the schedule today?" Lou asked.

"I've got to come up with some brilliant idea for the Paradisi bike." Tucker was building a name for her custom paint jobs on motorcycles and an occasional car or truck. Thanks to the popularity of shows like *American Chopper* and *Pimp My Ride,* her air-brushed murals, pictures and plain old pinstriping had taken more and more of her time away from the basic mechanic work.

She took a long sip of her coffee, knowing she needed caffeine in her system before she could come anywhere close to inspired.

She thought about the black custom bike that sat in her paint room as she appreciated a second sip. "Lou, you and the other guys start in on the appointments, okay? I'm going to head back to my office for an hour or so. I have some invoices to get out."

The only good thing about paperwork was that she hated it so much her mind frequently wandered and got creative in order to avoid doing it.

"Is your dad coming in today?" Lou asked.

"I'm sure he'll show up eventually." She offered what she hoped was a reassuring smile to Lou, but she couldn't be sure. She wasn't good at faking it—never had been. She needed to tell the guys the truth soon.

Soon, but not today.

"'Kay, Tuck," the older man said.

"Way to go, Tuck," she muttered to herself as she stomped to her office. She had to tell the guys sometime, but not until her dad was ready. And to date, George Tucker wasn't ready and she wasn't going to rush him. Lou knew the score without explanation and had pretty much taken over running the floor of the garage without being asked. And she'd taken over most of the hated paperwork. If her dad really did retire, she'd be doing it forever.

That was not the thought she wanted to start her day with, much less a week with.

She needed to speak to her dad about giving Lou a raise. Just one more thing on her to-do list. A list that no matter how hard she worked never seemed to get any shorter.

She slammed open her office door, her Monday mood really shot now, between Gary Johnson and Lou's innocent question about her father.

"Well, it's a hell of a thing when a man can't rely on his daughter's totally deluded happy Monday mood." Her father was sitting in a chair, his own cup of coffee in hand.

"What are you doing here, Pops?"

Her father looked so much better than he had a few months ago. Thanks to her very vigilant eye on his diet, he'd lost a few pounds, which the doctors said would help with his heart problems.

"Enjoying the view." He pointed at the bird feeder she'd mounted in the overgrown mulberry tree outside the window. "I never noticed the feeder before."

"I put it up years ago."

"I figured. It's got a weathered sort of look to it. Guess there are a lot of things I haven't noticed before. Sorry for that, kiddo."

"You noticed plenty, Pops."

"No. I missed some very big things, and even things I did notice—well, some I plain old ignored. Like the fact you were a girl. It was you, me and the guys at the shop. I treated you like one of them. I never pushed you to do girly things. If you'd had a mom, she'd have made sure you didn't spend all your time around men and car repairs."

Since her father had been sick, he'd had days of uncharacteristic nostalgia and occasionally, bouts of regret. Tucker wasn't sure what to do when he expressed such emotion, other than try to reassure him. "Pops, if I really wanted to do girly things, don't you think I would have done them? I mean, honestly, in my whole life, has anyone ever forced me to do something I didn't want to do, or managed to talk me out of something I did?"

"No. But the point is, I never gave you a chance to explore what you wanted. I kept you close and here you are in your thirties and still working at the garage. Still living in the same house."

Her father had bought a nice double-wide trailer and set it up next to the garage, leaving

15

the house across the street, where she'd grown up, for her and her son, Bart. "You could have stayed there and I could have gotten my own place."

"Not my point and you know it," he scolded. "I didn't want to stay there—but maybe you shouldn't have wanted to stay there either."

"Are you saying you want me to move?"

"Are you being deliberately obtuse, Angelina?" her normally affable father lashed out. "I don't want you to move and you know that I always wanted you to work at the shop with me. But I'm wondering now if I was selfish. Maybe all men reach an age where all they can do is look back and second guess their past decisions."

"Pops, is something wrong? Are you feeling short of breath, or having chest pains?" It was so hard to think of her once unstoppable father as ill and she hated it. She wanted him well again and back to his old self.

"No. I'm fine now, but I guess being sick leaves a man with a lot of time to think. I'm pushing seventy, and I won't be here forever. I'm worried about you."

Last Christmas the doctors had found blockage in her father's arteries and put a stent in. He'd come back to work, but not full-time. He'd wanted to, but she'd put her foot down. The doctor had told her that her father needed a lighter schedule, less stress and a better diet. She'd made it a point on trying to see he had all three, but she obviously hadn't done a good enough job if he was worried about her. "I'm fine, Pops. You have to know that I love my life."

"Yeah, but your life has always centered around the job, me and Bart. I'm here to tell you that I'm stepping back from the day-to-day operations of Tucker's Garage. Actually, that's a cop-out. I'm not only stepping back, I've decided that I'm retiring. Officially. I'm going to leave the business, along with the worries, in your capable hands. And Bart is going away to college in the fall. I guess, I'm concerned about where that's going to leave you."

Tucker looked at her father. Finding out her father was mortal shouldn't have come as a shock, but he'd always been so healthy, so much larger than life. His illness had scared her. He looked better now, but she couldn't help but worry. Having him retire from the business and take it easy would ease those worries a bit.

"I think it's a great idea, Pops. Me and the boys can handle things at the shop."

"We both know that you've been handling things for the last five months with no problem, other than there's been too much work for four people."

"And we're not complaining," she pointed out. "Given the economy, it's great that our business hasn't ebbed, but instead has exploded. The guys don't mind overtime, and I help in the garage as much as my schedule allows."

"A lot of that increased business has come from your end of things. You need to concentrate on the painting, not the repairs. And now that I'm officially retiring, you'll really have the business side of things to focus on, too."

"I can do it all." To be honest, she had a lot of time to work. Even though Bart was still here, he was wrapped up in his own life and enjoying the end of his senior year of high school, and she encouraged that. She'd been in her teens when she had him, and she wanted to give him all the moments she'd missed out on.

"Now that I've decided to retire, rather than just cut back, I think, more than ever, we should find someone to buy into the business," her father said.

"No." Since he'd been ill, he'd mentioned selling his half of the business to someone who could help them out. Someone who would have a vested interest in things. Tucker just shook her head. They'd had this conversation—well, fight actually—before. She didn't want some stranger having a say in the business she'd invested her blood, sweat and paint in, but she didn't want to upset her father by fighting about it again.

"We could let someone else buy in and do all those things you hate. The things I used to do," he tossed out, obviously hoping it would make the idea more appealing to her.

"No," she repeated, hoping her monosyllabic response would get her point across without another out-and-out argument that would send his blood pressure skyrocketing.

"I'd say we could hire someone, but I don't trust someone who *doesn't* have a vested interest. A partner would—"

"Pops, I'll find a way to make it all work out. It won't work with another partner." Hoping to soften her refusal, she added, "Once you've worked with the best, it's hard to settle for anyone else."

Her father sighed. "I'm not ruling the idea out, but we'll table it for now. That being said, I am making one last executive decision." Her father had that *look*.

Tucker would be hard pressed to define the *look* to an outsider, but as his daughter, she had no trouble recognizing it. There was a slight compression of his lips. The smallest flaring of his nostrils. He was squinting and reached up to pat his normally rumpled grey hair.

"What decision is that?" She was pretty sure that his look indicated that he thought it was a decision she wouldn't like. "Pops?"

"I hired someone."

"Pops, we've always done the hiring together." Even before she'd officially worked for her father, then with him as a partner, he'd had her sit in on interviews. He said he didn't want her forced to be around someone she didn't like.

"This one is special. I've known the guy for years and he really needed the work. And in the interest of honesty, he's got a record. White collar, six months in county, still on probation."

Tucker groaned. "Pops..." She didn't add anything to it because she knew it was pointless. When her father made his mind up, he was immovable. That's what his look said. *I'm a stone and you can't budge me. I won't change my mind.* So, she admitted defeat with grace. "When's he start?"

"Today. Told him to be in by eight-thirty. Wanted to talk to you and smooth things over before he showed up."

"Yeah, Pops, that's you, all smooth operatory."

Her father either didn't notice her sarcasm, or chose to ignore it as someone knocked on the door and he glanced at his watch. "Punctual. Gotta like that in a new employee," he said with a grin.

"Come on in," Tucker called. She expected to see some trouble-hardened man at the door, not... "Mr. Martinez?"

Tyler Martinez was one of the garage's best customers. He indulged in new vehicles like other people indulged in ice cream. High-end vehicles that fit well with his high-end designer suits, his dark good looks and his power job. But today, there was no designer suit, but rather a well worn pair of jeans and a white T-shirt that emphasized the fact the man worked out.

If the lines beneath his shirts were any indication, he'd been working out more than usual.

Not that she usually noticed.

Okay, so she noticed. A woman would have to be dead in order to ignore Tyler Martinez's sensual dark features. An image of a panther flashed through her mind and she almost laughed at how cliché that felt.

She pasted on her best business smile. Considering how much money and time Tyler spent at the shop it wouldn't do to be rude. "Mr. Martinez, I'm in a meeting. If you wouldn't mind waiting for a few minutes, I'll come get you and we can go over whatever your current vehicle requires."

"My current vehicle is a 2002 Ford F-150 that has seen better days, but I'm working on it myself, so it doesn't require any of the shop's services." Tyler frowned at her father. "You didn't tell her?"

"Doesn't pay to rush my Angelina," her father said with a trace of pride in his voice. "She comes around to things in her own time. I did tell her, only I hadn't told her who."

Tucker looked at Martinez, then at her father. Her mom-senses were tingling, something that normally only happened with Bart. "Told me?"

"Angel, meet Tucker's Garage's newest employee, Tyler Martinez."

"What the hell, Pops?" She turned to Tyler. "You don't work in a garage. You work for some fancy investment firm and wouldn't know a driveshaft from a piston."

Martinez frowned, his voice had a touch of gravel breaking in its normal whiskey smoothness. "Don't make assumptions about me, Angel." He dragged her name out, slow and intimate.

Maybe he thought she'd melt, but instead she felt fired up. "And don't call me Angel. It's Tucker, if you don't mind." Only her father called her Angelina or worse yet, Angel.

"I do mind, but since I'm an employee, my minding doesn't count. And to set your mind at ease, a driveshaft transmits torque, and a piston transfers force from the expanding gas to the cylinder—"

"You sound like a freakin' *Autos for Dummies* book." Tucker snorted. "I don't need an armchair mechanic, I need—"

"Angelina," her father snapped, "do you really think that I'd hire someone less than capable to work at the shop?"

She might fight with her father in private, but he rarely reprimanded her in public.

Rather than feel chagrined, she was more annoyed than ever. "Pops, it's obvious that there's a lot I don't know, isn't it? I mean, I came into work today and didn't know my father—my partner in the business—was quitting. And I

22

didn't know he's been interviewing potential employees without me and I didn't know—"

"Maybe I should leave the two of you to decide if I have a job, or not?" Without waiting for a response, Tyler Martinez left the office and shut the door softly behind himself.

"Now, see what you did, Pops?" Tucker said, feeling a mixture of frustration and embarrassment.

"Daughter, I don't want to have to pull rank, but..." He left the threat hanging there.

"You wouldn't." Annoyance beat out all the other emotions. "You've never tried to pull a father-knows-best on me since Bart's dad."

"And, I hate to say I told you so then, but..."

Frustration? This went beyond that. Tucker was pissed. Seriously pissed. And it was evident that so was her father. She'd tiptoed around him the last five months, but right now she ignored the fact he had a stent, as well as forgot she was trying to help him avoid stress. *"But...?"*

"Fine. You want me to finish my sentence?" he said, obviously as raring to fight as she was. "Let's try this. *But* I told you Bart's father was no good, and he was. He left you high and dry, and not to mention pregnant. You were only a teenager. A teenager who had to grow up too quick. I haven't had to play a father-knows-best card because you've lived your entire adult life cautiously. To the best of my knowledge, you've steered clear of any more good-looking men, and the men you do go out with don't last more than

23

a few dates at most. Well, Tyler's good looking and I know he's asked you out repeatedly in the past, but I also know he's a hell of a mechanic. Add to that, over the years, he's become a friend and he needed my help, so I gave it. Yeah, that means I'm sort of dumping him on you, *but* you need him."

"I don't need any man," Tucker sputtered.

"No, not like that. I mean, I like Tyler, but I want more than an ex-con for my daughter. No, he's not only a heck of a mechanic, but he's got experience handling people. Someone like that should take my place. Lou, Joe and North are great guys, but let's face it, articulate they ain't. Tyler is."

"I'm articulate, Pops. I can do more of the customer interaction if I need to."

"If you did, you'd be taking time away from your work, and let's face it, the garage has come to rely on your work. Your painting generates a lot of revenue. It's helped put us on the map. Hell, I'm a partner who's retiring, and I'm going to rely on you keeping us on the map. People come from states away to have you customize their cars and motorcycles. You're an artist, Angel, and that's what you need to focus on."

He rose slowly and suddenly looked haggard. "Trust me on this. Tyler will be good for the business."

Tucker's anger was replaced by concern. "You sure you're okay, Pops?"

"Fine. Now, I'm off to celebrate my retirement by going fishing, and I suggest that you go make nice with the new employee and introduce him around, then get started on the Paradisi bike."

She'd lost. Flat out lost. Most of the time, she'd continue the fight, but in the face of her father's ill health, she couldn't.

"Fine," she said with as much graciousness as she could muster. Her father's expression relaxed a bit and she knew that giving up the battle was worth it. She'd lose any fight, hire anyone, do anything to keep her father healthy and happy—to keep him with her as long as possible.

"And Angel?" her dad asked.

"Yeah, Pops?"

"I'm turning everything, from this moment on, over to you. I'm not saying we won't discuss the partner issue again, but I won't push it on you. As for Tyler, I not only wanted to help him out, I wanted to be sure that you weren't overwhelmed. I want you to have a life, Angel. I want you to be happy."

She got up and walked over to her father, then kissed his weathered cheek. "I'm happy, Pops. I only want you to be well."

"I'm feeling good today. It's almost summer, the sun is shining, and I'm going to spend my day out on the lake instead of working. That sounds like an excellent day to me."

She watched him walk slowly out of the office. Worrying about him still weighed on her and the sudden discovery that she was now the official managing partner of Tucker's Garage only added to it. The title seemed so much more serious than *acting* managing partner. That title had hinted at the possibility that eventually her father would be back at the helm.

It was time to realize that wasn't going to happen. But she couldn't think of what her father's official retirement implied. She had a new employee to meet and greet.

She'd spent months ducking Tyler Martinez's date invitations, and now she'd be working with him every day thanks to her father. That was a nasty way to start a week.

Normally, Mondays were her favorite day of the week. They were fresh and full of potential. But this Monday might go down as one of her worst ever on record.

TYLER WANTED TO get up and leave the garage for any number of very valid reasons, the most predominate of which was the fact Angelina Tucker had made it more than clear she wanted nothing to do with him.

A couple years ago, he'd spent months asking her out. She'd been kind with her refusals. She'd even tried some humor. But despite her kindness and humor, she'd made it abundantly clear she wasn't interested. Eventually, he'd stopped asking and they'd continued an amicable business relationship.

Well, today, it was very clear that she wasn't interested in having him work here either. In the past, his pride would have dictated him walking out. Now, he had no pride left. He needed a job, and since it was obvious he'd never be able to return to the investment firm, he only had one other skill to fall back on—auto mechanics.

All those years of bringing his vehicles to Tucker's Garage had made him proud. He was no longer the boy who had grease embedded under his nails. He knew how to repair and maintain his own vehicles, but he didn't have to.

The phrase *pride goes before the fall* played in his mind. He ignored it and repeated what had become his personal mantra of sorts. *The only constant in life is change.* His life was a prime example of that.

He stared out the window at the bucolic scene. The garage sat at the edge of Whedon, Pennsylvania, butting against farmland and woods. Through the copse of budding trees, Tyler could see the cows grazing without a care in the world.

Carefree—Tyler had never experienced that particular sensation. Given his current situation, he doubted he ever would.

"Mr. Martinez?"

He swung around and saw Angelina Tucker at the doorway. "If you'll come with me, I'll take you out to the shop and introduce you to the guys. I'm sure my father informed you that you'll be expected to be here at eight in the morning, and we work until five. Occasionally, a customer needs to pick up a car after that, and we take turns staying late. Of course, you'll be compensated for that. And you'll be expected to work every other Saturday, from eight until noon. Overtime for that, too. An hour for lunch. We try to stagger our lunches so someone's always in the shop. I think that's it. Any questions?"

She looked cute as she raked her fingers through her short, wild brown hair and rattled off the information. Of course, he'd never share the fact that he thought she was cute. Angelina wasn't interested in him when he'd had money and asked her out. He was pretty sure she'd be even less inclined to date him now. A prison record tended to turn most women off, and the ones it didn't, well, they weren't the type of woman who interested him anyway.

"Mr. Martinez?"

He realized he'd been staring at her without responding. "No, everything is perfectly clear to me. Thank you." She turned and left the room, obviously expecting him to follow. "And I'd like to thank you for taking a chance on me."

"My father's the one taking the chance. I'm hoping you prove worthy of it."

Tyler nodded. "I'll do everything in my power to."

"Fine."

She whisked him into the shop, introduced him to two older men, Joe and Lou, and a younger guy, North, who had a huge tattoo on his forearm.

"North?" he asked.

The kid grinned. "Yeah, my first day here, Lou said I was so far out I might as well be at the North Pole. The name sort of stuck." North caught Tyler's line of sight and shook his head. "Nah, it's not about the tat itself. Lou's is bigger than mine."

Lou snorted. "That's what all the girls say."

North laughed. "Well, his *tat* is bigger. No, they seemed to think the inspiration for my tat made me a bit out-there."

He held his forearm out to Tyler. Tyler recognized the Star Trek symbol above the words *Live Long and Prosper.*

"Some people," North looked pointedly at his coworkers, "seem to think having a Star Trek tattoo makes you a fringe element. Me, I say it means I boldly go forth. I kind of like the name anyway." He clapped Tyler's back. "Come on. You can help me today."

Tyler followed the kid, and as he walked away he heard Angelina say, "Keep an eye on him, guys. Make sure he learns his way around the shop."

He glanced back at Angelina and his pride reared its ugly head again. He wanted to go tell her to stick her job and her father's pity, but he needed this job and he was going to have to suck it up and deal with her.

"HEY, MOM."

Tucker glanced at the clock in her paint room and realized it was almost four o'clock. "Hey, Bart, how was school?"

She stood and stretched out the kinks that came from sitting crosslegged on the floor for so long. She should have put the motorcycle on a lift. She flexed her arms and fingers. She'd held the airbrush for too long.

"School was great. First final's on Monday and the rest come quickly after that. I'm planning on staying in most of the week and this weekend to start study."

She looked at her son and was, as always, amazed he was hers. Straight A student, good at sports, and cute to boot. Those were all great characteristics. But add to that, he was a nice kid.

He needed a haircut. He hadn't quite inherited her curls, but when his hair got too long, it fell into waves. She'd make him cut it before graduation.

It never ceased to amaze her that despite the fact she was little more than a kid herself when she had him, she'd managed to raise him to adulthood. She thought it was more a testament to how innately good her son was rather than anything she'd done.

"Nerd," she teased with good humored affection.

"Yeah, well, you live what you learn. You're the queen of hard work. Lou said that you didn't take a lunch break again and he suspects you were working after hours last night. I'm supposed to see to it that you pack it in and call it a day, even if it's early. And Grandpa said to come over to his house. He cooked."

Tucker realized her father's dinner invitation was a peace offering even as she groaned. "Oh, Bart, I'm so sorry. I'm a bad, bad mother. I mean, subjecting you to your grandfather's cooking is nothing short of torture."

"Hey, it's okay. He went to Wegman's and bought some macaroni salad and there's tossed salad to go with the steak he's grilling."

"Phew." She wiped her brow with exaggerated relief. "Oh, why didn't you say so? That's edible and qualifies me for at least fair-to-middling mom."

Bart kissed her cheek. "I think you're higher than that. Not much maybe, but higher than middling," he joked. "Come on, let's go get you fed."

Tucker got up off the floor and studied the bike. It had an RC car on it. Not her first choice for painting, but Mr. Paradisi had three great loves: his motorcycle, his RC car club and his family. He said the pecking order changed daily. "What do you think?"

"I think the Paradisis will be thrilled. You made an RC car look cool. And I love how you worked the gas cap into the remote control picture."

"Yeah, I thought that was inspired, too. "

They walked out to the front garage and Lou slapped Bart's back. "Figured you'd talk her out of her hidey-hole. Now, on to supper, boy."

Tucker loved seeing the guys interact with her son. Bart might not have had a father in the picture growing up, but he had her father, and the guys at the shop. It seemed to be enough for him.

He grinned at the older man. "Sure thing, Lou."

"Hey, how's the new guy?" Tucker asked.

"He did a great job today. Knows his way around cars, that's for sure."

Tucker couldn't help but wonder why a guy who knew his way around cars felt the need to have someone else service his vehicles all these years. Even things as simple as new spark plugs or oil changes. It didn't make sense. She glanced at her son. "Let me check in with him, then we can go. Want to meet him?"

"Sure."

She found Tyler Martinez underneath a 1953 Volkswagen Beetle. She'd always referred to him as Mr. Martinez when he was a customer, but now that he was an employee, that sounded odd, so she called, "Tyler?"

His creeper zipped out from under the car and Tyler smiled for a minute, then his expression froze when he spotted her. "Yes?"

"I wanted to introduce you to my son. Spencer Tucker, otherwise known as Bart, this is Tyler Martinez, the garage's newest employee."

"You can call me Spencer," Bart told him. "Everyone in the real world does...it's only here in Mom's mystic workplace that my childhood nickname still haunts me."

"That's because you are not a Spencer," Tucker assured him. She enjoyed falling into their old argument. "I mean, I thought you were when you were born. I looked down and thought, *Spencer.* But I was wrong. You're a Bart, through and through."

"And that, Mr. Martinez, is why you might as well call me Bart, too. Because Mom will pretend not to know who you're talking about if you call me Spencer. Just like she doesn't know who you're talking to if you call her *Angelina.*" He singsonged her name and laughed as she scowled.

"And that's the problem with giving babies names at birth. They're not fully developed. They're tiny little blobs of humanity. A good name—a true name—tends to become apparent within the first few years. I'm Tucker, he's Bart. Do you have a nickname?"

"No. Tyler is fine."

Tucker noted that Tyler wasn't enjoying her banter with Bart. His face was frozen into an expression of polite interest, but it was apparent he was anything but.

Not for the first time, she felt foolish in front of him. "Well, we're heading out. See you in the morning."

"Yes, ma'am."

"Tucker," she assured him. "Not ma'am."

"Or Angelina," Bart said, still kidding around.

"No." She tossed her son a motherly glare of warning. "It's simply Tucker."

"Tucker," Tyler parroted. "See you tomorrow morning, Tucker."

"Come on, Bart. Let's go get something to eat, I'm starved." She clapped her hand on her son's back, and for a moment, she thought she caught the ghost of a smile on Tyler's face, but it happened so fast, she couldn't be sure. His face was once again expressionless as he gave her a nod, then slipped again under the car.

"He seems nice, Mom," Bart said.

"Yeah, he seems nice, but meeting someone for a minute doesn't give us enough information to really discover if they're nice or not. It takes—"

"Another Mom-lecture, ladies and gentlemen," Bart teased. "You know, I have friends whose parents wallop them when they make a mistake. Sometimes I wonder if that's preferable to being lectured to death."

"That wasn't a lecture," she protested.

"No, that was your chance to work in one of your famous life lessons, and those are so close to lectures, it's hard to tell the difference."

She playfully slugged his arm. "Well, you can rest assured I can wallop you if the lectures don't work."

Bart laughed. "Oh, Mom, you try to be tough. And I imagine there are many people who believe you are, but no one who knows you would believe that for an instant. And I know you, Mom. You're a marshmallow."

"Take that back. I work in a garage full of guys and I am not a marshmallow."

"Oh, yeah. You're like a great big candy bar. Crunchy on the outside, and all soft or mushy on the inside. Maybe that'll be your new nickname... Candy." He sprinted across the yard toward her father's, hollering "Candy" over his shoulder.

"I'll show you how tough I can be," she shouted, taking off after him, laughing for the sheer joy of laughing.

And at that moment, chasing after her son as they both teased each other and laughed, Tucker decided it wasn't such a bad Monday after all.

CHAPTER TWO

Two weeks.

Tucker stared at the calendar hanging on the wall next to her desk and was struck by the fact that it had already been two weeks since Tyler Martinez had started working at the shop. He was, on paper, the perfect employee. He was the first one to arrive every morning, and the last one to leave every night. He knew as much about cars as anyone in the shop. He got along with everyone, never caused a problem.

But...

Yes, there was a *but* dangling there at the end of her thoughts.

Tucker tried to put a finger on it. Tyler wasn't standoffish. He joked around with the guys, and they all seemed to accept him. He didn't actually joke around with her, but he was polite.

No, standoffish wasn't the word she wanted. Maybe, *closed book* was a better description of Tyler Martinez.

Back when her friend Eli was expecting her son and having man troubles of her own, Tyler had actively pursued Tucker. Tucker had said no, of course. After all, Tyler was a successful businessman, and she worked in a garage. He was a carefree bachelor, she was a mother. He wore designer suits, she wore jeans. They had no common ground.

Maybe day-to-day proximity had convinced him that they weren't meant to be anything more than a boss and employee. Or maybe prison had changed him. Whichever it was, the man she remembered was gone.

And if he didn't want to nag her for dates anymore, that was fine with her. She wasn't looking to date him, though she wished he wouldn't treat her as if she had a case of playground cooties. Even when she'd said no to dates, he'd laughed off her refusals and told her he'd simply keep trying until she said yes. He'd been open and engaging back then, and somewhere between then and now, he'd closed up tight.

Tucker forced herself to concentrate on payroll in front of her. She didn't have time to ponder the mystery of Tyler Martinez. She went back to tallying hours and calculating checks, when the sound of voices pulled her from her math. She stared out her window, past the mulberry tree, and at the edge of the building she saw Tyler and some tall blond guy.

She couldn't make out more than a murmuring of voices, but it was obvious it was a serious conversation. The stranger's voice rose enough for Tucker to hear, "It's done, Tyler. You can't undo it. They know the truth."

Tyler's voice rose as well. Tucker could hear the utter frustration in it as he said, "A father's name is the most important thing he can pass on to his son. Hell, you literally passed on your name. Jason Emerich Matthews, Junior. Let that mean something to him."

"I want it to. That's why I'm doing this. I want my name to mean something. I want Jace to know his father made a mistake—it might have been for all the right reasons, but it was still wrong. I need him to know that I was willing to own up to it and pay the consequences." The blond guy turned and walked around the corner of building, out of Tucker's line of sight.

"Jason," Tyler called and followed him.

What was that all about? Tucker wandered into the garage at the same time Tyler slammed the door and strode over to a workbench.

"What's going on?" she asked Lou, jerking her head in Tyler's direction.

The old man shrugged. "Some guy came by, asked for Tyler and they went outside. Whatever they were talking about, it obviously didn't go well."

Part of Tucker wanted to see if Tyler was okay, but she suspected he wouldn't appreciate her concern.

Even from across the shop, she could see the tension practically radiating from him in the way he held himself—stiff and unapproachable. "Right. Holler if you need anything."

Lou nodded and went back to a car on the lift. Tucker went back to payroll, anxious to finish so she could get back to the paintroom and determined not to think about the garage's newest employee. He did his work well, and that's all that should concern her.

She wondered why it wasn't.

Two days later after Jason's visit to the garage, Tyler's phone buzzed in his pocket.

In his old life, his phone rang nonstop. These days it was mostly silent. Old friends avoided him like the plague, as if doing a stint in County was contagious. As if they were afraid they'd develop a sudden yearning to wear orange jumpsuits. As if they'd never been his friend at all.

Well, that was fine with Tyler. He didn't need them. He knew who his friends were— strike that—who his friend, *singular*, was. One was more than enough.

Jason was more than a friend, he was like a brother. Tyler knew he'd do anything for him, and vice versa.

His phone buzzed again, and since he was in the middle of eating lunch, he pulled it out and checked to see who it was.

Jason.

"Jason, what's up?"

"Mr. Martinez?" a woman's voice said.

"Yes?"

"This is Jessica Ahearn at St. Vincent's. There's been an accident..." The woman explained she was a nurse, that Jason was in an accident and Tyler's number was under ICE in his cellphone.

"Ice?" Tyler asked, because it was easier to ask a question than to have the nurse tell him things he didn't want to hear.

"*In case of emergency—ICE.* Mr. Matthews's car hit an embankment. He's in surgery now."

Tyler had barely processed the thought of Jason being in an accident when he remembered the baby. "Jace?"

"He's in surgery," she repeated.

"No, Jace. His son. A baby. Was he in the car?"

"Only Mr. Matthews was transported here, sir."

"I need the names of the guys in the ambulance, or the police, or..." Jace's sitter. He knew her name. He couldn't think of it. He knew her name.

"Pam."

"Pam?" the woman repeated.

"That's the babysitter's name. I'm going to call her. Could you check with the ambulance crew and call me back. I'm on my way."

"Sure, I'll do that, Mr. Martinez."

"I'm in Whedon. I'll be at the hospital in under a half hour." Tyler had always thought the half hour distance between Erie and Whedon wasn't bad, but suddenly it was too far. He needed to be there now.

"Mr. Martinez, he'll be in surgery for hours. If I find out anything about the baby, I'll call right away."

"Thank you, Ms. Ahearn."

Tyler hurried over to his coworker. "Lou, I need to leave early. It's a family emergency. I'll make up the hours, or you can dock my pay, or hell, fire me if you have to. I've got to go."

The old guy had been decent to Tyler, so had everyone else at the garage, so it came as no surprise when he said, "Don't talk crazy, kid. You go do what you have to. Can I do anything to help?"

"No. I'll handle it. But I'm not sure when I'll be back in."

"Go do what you have to," Lou repeated. "We'll manage."

Tyler ran to his car and tried to think as he headed toward the interstate. What the hell was Pam's last name? He'd met the woman the few times he'd picked up the baby for Jason and Mellie before he'd gone to County.

No matter how hard he tried, he couldn't remember her last name. Why hadn't he ever thought to get her name and number from Jason?

He decided to drive to her house and see if Jace was there, then he'd go to the hospital.

Shit, he had to call Jason's mom and dad, too. They'd moved to Florida when they retired.

Heartsick, he called their number as he barreled down I-79 toward Erie and told them what little he knew. "I'll call as soon as I talk to the doctors," he promised.

"I'm making arrangements for the earliest flight I can get," Jason's father promised.

Neither of them asked the question that was hanging around like a white elephant in the room. What if Jace had been in the car with his father?

Tyler drove faster than he should have, but hopefully not fast enough to attract police attention. The last thing he needed was to be pulled over by the cops and questioned. He was still on parole, and while he didn't think a speeding violation would send him back to jail, he wasn't sure and he couldn't afford to take the chance. He had to be there for Jason.

He drove slowly up the big hill and into the babysitter's drive, praying that Jace was there. He felt sick to his stomach as he knocked on the door. Pam opened the door, Jace on her hip.

"I'm not sure you remember me—" he started.

She interrupted. "I definitely remember you, Mr. Martinez." Her words were said with that certain tone that let him know exactly how she felt about criminals darkening her doorstep.

"Jason was in an accident and I didn't have your number and was praying Jace was here." He held his hand out to the baby. Pam hesitated a moment, then handed him over.

Tyler inhaled the scent of clean baby and had the first bit of relief he'd felt since the phone call from the nurse. "Jason's in surgery and I need to be at the hospital. But I had to know Jace was safe first. Can you keep him?"

The woman's expression softened. "I wish I could, Mr. Martinez, but we're leaving town tonight and driving to Cleveland in order to catch our plane tomorrow. Jason knew I couldn't watch Jace for the next two weeks. He said he'd made arrangements."

"All right," Tyler said, his mind racing as he tried to figure out what to do. "I know Jason told you I have permission to take Jace, so I'll do that now and sort something out. Can you get his things?"

Minutes later, Pam brought over the baby's diaper bag in his carseat and handed him a piece of paper. "That's my cell number. I am sorry about Jason. Will you call me and let me know how he is?"

"I will," he promised, juggling Jace, the carseat and diaper bag. What the hell should he do now? Rush to be with Jason? But he knew his friend would insist the baby was Tyler's priority. He felt torn in two. He needed someone responsible. Someone he could trust to watch Jace.

Suddenly an image of Angelina Tucker flashed through his head. The day she'd introduced him to her son, the way they teased each other with such ease and comfort. As he finished strapping the baby's carseat into his truck, he found himself heading toward the small auto shop on the outskirts of Whedon.

Angelina might tell him no, that she wasn't watching the baby for him, but he had to try. She was pretty much his only option.

The short drive back to the garage seemed to take forever, but he finally arrived, parked the truck in front and juggled Jace and all his accouterments into the shop. "Tucker still here?" he asked.

Lou, North and Joe all eyed the baby, but none of them asked any questions. Lou nodded toward the paint room. "She's in there."

"Thanks."

He opened the door, and unwilling to take the baby into the paint fumes, called in, "Angelina, can I see you a minute?"

She came out, wiping her hands on a rag and saying, "I thought Lou said you had some emergency." She stopped as she saw the baby. "That's a baby."

"Yes. Can you watch him? I don't know anyone else who knows anything about babies— not anyone I would trust him with. Will you do it?"

"Yes, but—" was as far as Tucker got. At the first word, Tyler thrust the towheaded baby into her hands and took off at a run, yelling behind him, "I'll call you."

"What's his name?" she hollered.

He stopped, turned around and said, "Jace. He's my godson. His father's in the hospital." And with that, he was gone.

It had been a very long time since Bart was anywhere near this small, but Tucker held the baby with surprising ease. Like riding a bike, it came back.

Lou, North and Joe poked their heads around the corner. "So what's that all about?"

"Tyler's the baby's godfather, and the baby's dad is in the hospital. I don't know much more than that, other than the baby's name is Jace. So for now, it looks like I have a baby. Would someone go clean up my mess in the paint room while I take Jace to the house?"

"Sure, Tuck," Lou said, then nodded to North who bustled past her to the room. "He said there was a family emergency?"

Tucker shrugged. "I don't know anything else. I'm sure he'll explain later. Whatever's going on, Tyler is shaken. For now, I'll let you guys take care of the rest of the afternoon here and I'll take the munchkin home, unless someone would like to trade off?"

Lou and Joe shook their heads and hurried back to their repairs. "Looks like it's you and me, kid."

She hauled everything across the lot to her house. It was a small ranch that still had most of the furniture she'd grown up with. She'd thought about updating the furnishings, but she liked the

Ethan Allen hardwood pieces, and never felt anything more than a new couch was required. She'd bought a new one about four years ago, and it was oversized and covered in a brown micro material that was wearing like iron. She put the baby and his stuff on it.

He immediately began to wiggle and squirm. She helped him lower himself to the floor, and watched as he toddled off to explore her living room. She made a quick sweep of the room and possible dangers, but it looked pretty good to her, so she went back to the bag as she kept half an eye on Jace. "So, let's see what we have in here." There was one dirty romper, two diapers, some wipes, a half eaten plastic container of Cheerios, some powered toddler formula. "Well, I think first thing on our list is some shopping. This won't last you long."

Bart charged into the house, spotted her and the baby sitting on the floor looking through a magazine as if he could read. "What is that?"

"That is a baby."

Bart's expression said that he didn't think his mother was as funny as she thought she was. "Yeah, Mom, I know it's a baby, but whose baby is it?"

"That I don't know. I do know he's Tyler's godson and there's no one else to watch him because his dad's in the hospital, so he's in my care until Tyler gets back."

Bart approached the baby and studied him as if studying some alien life-form.

Tucker realized how little interaction her son had with children. Since her friend Eli Keller had a son, then adopted a daughter, Bart had a bit more experience with little kids, but he'd grown up an only child and had never dealt with a baby for more than the occasional dinner at Eli's in-laws, the Kellers. When Eli joined the family, the Kellers promptly enveloped Tucker, Bart and her dad, too. Tucker had coined the term Kellerized to explain the way the family informally adopted people.

"He's sort of cute," Bart finally said.

"He's also almost out of diapers and given that he has teeth, he's probably in need of some solid food, as well as more formula. This might have lasted him at the sitter's, but there's no telling how long we'll have him, so we should have more. I need to do some power-shopping for him. Wanna come with?"

Bart still warily eyed the baby. "He looks like he's going to cry."

"He probably needs his diaper changed and a quick bottle. Then we'll all go get the essentials."

Bart frowned. "Shopping and a baby. You do know how to show me a good time, Mom."

Tucker chuckled and she stripped the baby down. "That's a mother's job, kid."

Two hours later, Bart was on the floor rolling a truck for Jace, who laughed out loud each time Bart said, "Zoom."

Tucker had gone to the store planning to buy the essentials, but in the end, had bought some toys and books as well. Watching Bart with Jace, she didn't regret the added expense. Both the *boys* were having fun. Bart would have made a great big brother. She felt a not unfamiliar spurt of guilt for her son's unconventional upbringing. He'd been born to a teen mother, and had only had the minimal contact with his biological father. She'd never married, and though she dated on occasion, she had a strict policy of never allowing Bart to meet any of the men. At first because she feared a revolving group of men would be confusing to him, and later because that's how it had always been.

Tucker was enjoying the Bart and Jace show when her cell phone rang. A number she didn't recognize showed up on the caller ID. "Hello?"

"Tucker, it's me, Tyler."

"How are you?"

"I'm fine. It's Jace's father. It doesn't look good." Tyler's voice broke as he said the words. "I'll try to be there as soon—"

"Don't be an ass. Stay with your friend. I can handle the baby."

"I couldn't—"

"Unless something's changed since you dropped him off with me, you not only can, you sort of have to. I've been a mother my entire

48

adult life. I have exactly two skills in this life—cars and kids. I'll watch Jace for as long as you need me to. Stay with your friend."

"But I don't even know if Jace has enough stuff. I just took what the sitter handed me. I should have thought—"

Tucker cut him off. "I took care of it already. Don't worry about Jace. Worry about the kid's father. Call if you need anything else." She disconnected before he could argue.

"Is he coming?" Bart asked.

Tucker shook her head. "It's Jace's dad. I don't have all the particulars, but for now, he's ours."

Bart rolled the truck toward Jace, who giggled. "He's not so bad."

She looked at her son, no longer a boy, but a man. In a few months, he'd take off for college. She wasn't sure what she'd do without him. She'd been younger than he was now when she'd had him. It had always been the two of them. The two of them and her dad. And the guys at the shop. Now, her dad was retiring and Bart was off to start his own life. Where did that leave her?

"Mom, you have that sort of spacey, sappy look on your face. Again," Bart added for emphasis. "You're thinking about me leaving home."

"No, I wasn't," she denied. "I was thinking about how I'm going to get Werner's car ready. He was coming by first thing in the morning for it, and Tyler was the one working on it."

"I could watch the runt while you go finish it," Bart offered. "Which was, by the way, I know what you were hoping I'd say."

Tucker chuckled. "You are a smart boy. I shouldn't be long, but I hate to have a customer show up for a car that's not ready. And there's an added benefit of you watching a kid and finding out it's not a cake-walk—"

Bart's groaned interrupted her. "Seriously, you're going to turn me helping you out by watching this kid into some teen-parent-prevention lesson?"

Tucker laughed. "An inventive parent works with the opportunities life gives them."

"You're wacked, Mom, but that's one lesson you've driven home without me watching the baby." He made a shooing motion. "So, get, I've got it, Mom. I'll call if me and the kid have problems."

She started to the door, then turned back. "You've got his toys, his food and the new books."

"You bought out half the store. We've got plenty. Go."

"Fine. I'll hurry."

Tucker wasted no time climbing under the car that was still waiting for Tyler. She was sure the other guys would have finished it. One of them would have come back tonight, or come in early tomorrow if she asked, but she wanted to do it. It wasn't much, but it made her feel as if she was doing something for Tyler. Something tangible.

When he'd been a customer and asked her out, he'd had an aura of self-confidence. He believed the world was his oyster and even her rejections couldn't dent his self-image. That Tyler Martinez had known he had the world in the palms of his hands, and it didn't seem to occur to him that his belief in that basic fact could change.

This new Tyler seemed to be getting kicked over and over again. He'd lost his career and his good name when he went to jail. And remembering his expression when he showed up with the baby, he was terrified he was going to lose his friend.

Well, she couldn't do anything to help his friend, or get his old life back for him, but she could watch Jace and she could damn well fix this car.

It wasn't much, but it would have to be enough.

She started checking where Tyler had left off with the Werners' car.

She knew Bart would call if he had problems.

She smiled because he'd caught on to her master plan. Taking care of a baby was a better life lesson than any of her lectures could be. Kids were hard work. Maybe watching Jace would help Bart remember that when he went off to college.

She decided that taking her time on the car was not such a bad idea after all, because being a grandmother in her thirties was definitely not on her list of future plans.

Of course, she wasn't quite sure what those were, but she trusted that eventually she'd figure it out.

THREE DAYS LATER, Tyler dragged himself out of his truck and onto Angelina's porch. He rang the doorbell and waited.

She'd been amazing, and he wasn't sure why. She'd not only kept Jace, but with the help of her father and son, she'd juggled the baby's care with work. She assured him that it was fine, that she knew he needed to be with his friend.

She hadn't pushed him for explanations on his friendship with Jason. She hadn't asked him for anything.

Tyler had spent the last three days waiting for Jason to wake up, but his friend had slowly gone from bad to worse. When Jason's parents had arrived from their retirement community in Florida, Tyler had felt stretched almost beyond his limits as he tried to support them. Jason was their only son and they were crushed.

When the end came, it had been swift. There was no fanfare. No final moments with poignant words. One minute, Jason had been breathing—still clinging to life. The next minute he simply stopped—stopped breathing, stopped living. Mrs. Matthews had totally fallen apart. It was all he could do to help Mr. Matthews get her to

Jason's house where they were staying. Her grief was tangible.

Tyler pushed his own pain aside. The Matthews had done so much for him. He'd do what he had to in order to support them. Later, he'd grieve on his own.

He told them he'd bring the baby over later in the day and that he'd help them plan Jason's funeral.

Tyler realized he hadn't felt the full impact of Mellie's death because he'd been in prison. Jason had called and told him when she'd died, but there hadn't been anything Tyler could do. She wasn't a blood relation, so there wasn't even a possibility of being released for her funeral. He'd suffered through the loss on his own.

This time, he wasn't alone. He'd thought it would hurt less if he was with others who shared his pain, but watching people he loved suffering made it hurt more.

He waited at Angelina's door, pushing down his hurt.

The door flew open. "Tyler?"

"He's gone. Jason's dead." It was the first time he'd said the words out loud and they struck him. "He's gone."

Angelina reached out, grabbed his hand and tugged him inside. "I'm so sorry, Tyler. What can I do?"

Angelina's warm reaction didn't exactly surprise him, but it didn't mean he understood it, either. "I came to get Jace." His mind was muddled; he accepted her concern, but he knew he couldn't impose on Angelina any further.

Rather than go get the baby, she asked, "When's the last time you slept or ate?"

"What day is it?" he asked.

"Saturday."

The days had blurred together and he didn't have a clue. "I don't know."

"You can crash in my room and I'll take care of him for a little while longer. He's a good kid."

"Angel, I can't—"

He thought of her as Angelina, or Angel. Back when he'd had the world in his hand, he'd called her that, but everything had changed since then. He knew he should call her Tucker, like everyone else, but she didn't notice, or simply didn't correct his slipup as she interrupted him. "You're right. You can't do much of anything until you get some sleep and some food. In that order." She led him down the hall. "And a shower."

She sniffed the air. "Maybe the shower first."

"I—"

She led him to her room and gave him a gentle push inside. "The bathroom's right through that door. There are clean towels in the cupboard. Take a shower, then go to bed, Tyler. We'll figure it all out when you get up."

He was too exhausted to argue. He took a shower and used the shampoo that was out. It smelled flowery. It smelled like Angelina. Until now, he'd never noticed that despite her work clothes, she'd always smelled very feminine.

He wrapped a clean towel around his waist, went into her room and climbed in Angelina Tucker's bed. The last thing his foggy brain registered is that the bed smelled flowery, too.

It smelled like Angelina.

That thought comforted him as he fell asleep.

TUCKER WAITED A HALF hour, then tiptoed into the bathroom through the hall door and picked up Tyler's clothes. She planned on washing them while he slept. She couldn't swear to it, but she was pretty sure the jeans and tight black t-shirt were the same ones he'd had on three days ago when he'd brought her Jace. The door to the bedroom was cracked and she saw Tyler sprawled on her bed.

A towel was still wrapped around his hips, but his chest and legs were bare. She felt something stirring, something that hadn't stirred for a very long time.

It wasn't that she was immune to men. It was simply that she didn't have a lot of opportunity to meet men. She lived her life in a man's world, but it sometimes felt as if there were no men she could, or would, be interested in. And when she did meet a man, she frequently couldn't get rid of them quick enough. It wasn't that some weren't nice—they were. It was simply that fitting anything more than an occasional date into her busy life didn't work for her. She wasn't interested in long-term. She'd have thought that would make her their dream woman. But it seemed to do the opposite. The more she said she wasn't interested, the more they pursued her.

Instantly, she realized she was ogling a man who'd lost a friend and was obviously devastated. She felt ashamed and rushed from the room, tossed his clothes in the washer and went to see if Jace was awake yet.

She found him sitting in the portable baby crib she'd bought.

"Hi, little man. Let's go get some breakfast."

Taking care of the baby was enough of a distraction that she could ignore the fact there was a half-naked man in her bed.

Well, not ignore, but almost ignore.

She was not going to think about the fact that she'd thought Tyler Martinez looked very good in a tight black t-shirt, and now she'd discovered he looked even better out of it.

CHAPTER THREE

Tyler woke up disoriented.

Where was he?

It was the scent that finally triggered his memory. He was in Angelina Tucker's bed. On the heels of that realization came another—Jason was dead. He needed to get the baby and go check on Jason's parents.

Tyler found his clothes in a neat pile in the bathroom. They'd obviously been laundered.

He added that to the long list of things Angelina had done for him as he dressed.

He went looking for his benefactor and found her in the living room on the floor stacking blocks with Jace. He stood in the doorway, mesmerized by the sight. She'd stack a small tower and Jace would whack it over, then laugh hysterically as she'd sputter, "Why you..." and rebuild it, only to have it toppled again.

She spotted him and smiled. "You woke up."

"I did and found some clean clothes. Thank you."

She seemed flustered by his gratitude and shrugged. "It was self-preservation. They practically walked to the washer and begged to be cleaned." She grew serious. "I'm sorry about your friend."

"Thank you. He was more than a friend..." Tyler stopped, not sure how to describe his relationship with Jason and his parents. There was the family he'd been born into, such as they were, and then there were the Matthews, the family he'd chosen...or rather the family who'd chosen him.

"Your friend's got a great kid. I figured Jace's parents were pretty special. I'm sorry he's lost his father."

"Mellie, his mom, is gone, too. Jace only has his grandparents left."

"I'm sorry for that, too." Tucker shook her head. "But you're wrong. He has you."

Jace deserved better than him. Lucky for the kid he had Jason's parents, who were the best. They were two of the most decent people he'd ever known. "His grandparents will take care of him. Speaking of which, I need to take him to them. We've got to make the funeral arrangements." He paused. "About work...?"

"Don't worry. Dad cleared your absence with your parole officer, and your job is waiting for you after the funeral. Will you call me with the details?"

Her question brought him up short. "Why?"

Tucker shook her head, sending her short curls flying. "So we can come and show our respect."

58

"You didn't know him." She'd never even met Jason or his parents, so he didn't understand.

"No, but we know you. You work for us. We want to be there for you. That's what friends do." Her expression didn't brook any arguments.

Tyler hadn't understood Angelina back when he'd asked her out and she'd said no, despite the fact he was pretty sure she wanted to say yes. He didn't think he was being conceited when he thought she was as attracted to him as he was to her. He understood her even less now. He simply said, "Thanks." He leaned down to the baby. "Hey, Jace."

Jace immediately held up his hands to be lifted.

"He's not shy about what he wants." Angelina laughed as Tyler picked up the baby. "Bart has begun referring to us as Jace's minions. He's got everyone at the shop totally under his thumb."

"I don't know how to thank you both. To thank everyone at the shop for picking up the slack for me."

"Like I said, helping out—that's what we do. You should have seen him with North. North's got a Star Trek phaser app on his phone and was thrilled that Jace thought it was as cool as he did. The rest of us simply mock it, but Jace and North played with that thing for more than a half hour. I'm afraid that first it's going to be phaser apps on a phone, and next thing you know, North will be taking Jace to ComicCon, or DragonCon."

Jason had been a huge science fiction buff who'd kept trying to tempt Tyler into joining him by giving him books or DVDs to watch. Tyler realized that his friend would never again rave about how brilliant *Buffy the Vampire Slayer* was, or threaten to give him *a Star Wars* ringtone.

He noticed Angelina was still talking. "...and Lou and my dad took turns playing honorary grandpa with him. They were talking about taking him fishing. I put a stop to that. I figured I'd fail as babysitter if I let him become fish-bait. But I'm sure they'll be asking to borrow him sometime. They used to take Bart."

Tyler didn't know what to say. He was an ex-con, but no one at Tucker's garage seemed to notice. They simply accepted him as one of their own. "Angel, I—"

"Tucker, remember, Ace?" She smiled as she said the words.

Without thinking, Tyler leaned down and kissed her. It started out as a quick buss on the cheek, but she turned her head, and his lips were on hers. It was a tender kiss of friendship that quickly turned into something more. Something Tucker actively participated in and then abruptly pulled back from, looking flustered. He didn't wait for her to holler at him, he simply took the baby and walked to where he'd spotted Jace's carseat.

"Don't forget his diaper bag," Tucker said, following after him, bag in hand.

He started toward his truck.

"Thanks. I seem to be thanking you a lot."

"We look out for each other. No thanks expected."

He knew she meant that—she didn't require or expect gratitude. She didn't even recognize how extraordinary that was.

He looked at the small woman in her holey jeans and a t-shirt that had a motorcycle on it and read *Ride It Like You Stole It*. Her hair was a mass of crazy curls and she didn't have a bit of makeup on. All that being said, she was beautiful and everything in him wanted nothing more than to kiss her again.

But he didn't. He felt guilty for wanting to. After all, his best friend was dead. How could he be thinking about women when Jace was gone? It said something about him, he admitted as they agreed to switch vehicles and fished his truck key out of his pocket for Tucker. "I'll call later on."

"Okay." She stood in front of him for a minute, as if weighing something in her head, then moved swiftly and kissed his cheek.

Before he could do or say something that would totally unman himself, Tyler got in Angelina's black Pilot and headed back into Erie, where Jason's parents were waiting.

He glanced at the baby in the rearview mirror. Jace was chortling a string of noncoherent syllables to himself, happy and content. Tyler caught the word *Da*, and felt choked up. He remembered the day Jason had called him to tell him Mellie was pregnant. The baby didn't know he'd lost everything.

But Tyler did and his heart ached for him. For Jason's parents.

And, though it made him feel small to think it, for himself.

Jason Matthews stood up for Tyler and stood by Tyler. Jason had given him the closest thing to a family that he was ever going to have.

And now he was gone.

Tyler felt totally alone, but then he remembered Angelina's simple assurance that they were there for him.

The thought warmed him and helped him feel as if he was able to get through these next few days. He had to bury his friend, then he had to say goodbye to his godson when the Matthews took the baby back to Florida with them.

But he wasn't totally alone.

And Tyler Martinez was a man who recognized how much that was worth.

It was worth everything.

Tucker walked into the Kloecker Funeral Home along with her father, Lou, Joe and North. The place was filled with people who'd grouped together sharing tears and stories of the deceased. She spotted a man and woman who had to be Jason's parents. The woman held a cane in one hand, and Jace in the other. They were surrounded by people offering their sympathies. Tyler was nowhere to be seen. She scanned the crowds and finally spotted him in a corner, standing by himself. His expression unreadable. His posture was ramrod stiff, and his fists were clenched at his side as he stared out the window.

Rather than get in the line of people waiting to pay their respects with her father and the guys, she walked over to Tyler. "How're you doing?" She heard the words come out of her mouth and wished she could suck them back in. "Sorry. Dumb question."

Tyler offered her a weak smile. "I'm as okay as I can be."

"Why are you hiding back here?" She noticed that people kept glancing at them, and cut Tyler a wide berth, as if he had something contagious.

"Not hiding, simply staying out of the way." His voice was tight, contained. Too controlled.

"Come with me." She took his hand and pulled him toward the door. People parted as they approached. She saw her dad send her a questioning look, but she shook her head and trusted he knew that she meant she had it under control. She continued leading Tyler until they were far enough outside the funeral home, at the far end of the parking lot. No one could overhear.

"Spill."

"I'm fine," Tyler repeated.

"Ty, we both work on cars and we know that systems need to be vented or else the pressure builds until it blows up. Your pressure's building. Vent." He still didn't say anything, so she pressed. "Jason was a friend. I never saw you two together, but it's obvious you were a good friend to him. So why is everyone in there treating you like you have leprosy?"

Tyler sighed. "Those people are former colleagues. And it seems that they don't take kindly to ex-cons who went away for embezzling from their firm."

"Did you do it?" She wasn't sure why she'd asked, but once the words were out of her mouth, she very much wanted to hear Tyler's answer.

Rather than answer, he simply said, "What?"

"Did you do it? You said you went to prison for it, but you didn't say you did it. There's a difference. I caught it."

"You're the first person to ask me that question."

"So, did you do it?" She wasn't sure why she was so sure, but she was. There was more to the story than Tyler simply embezzling money from his firm. He'd had money. At least enough money for high-end cars and suits and such. So why?

His jaws clenched. "I'm not going to talk about it."

"Fine. Then talk about Jason. How long did you know him?"

"We grew up together. Not in the same neighborhood, but we went to the same school. I was in high school and the first day our freshman year, our science teacher partnered us. Jason was lost when it came to science, so I helped him. I was behind in English, so he helped me. We were both horrible at French, but we met this girl, Mellie DeDioniso and she got us both through four years of that. All I remember about French is how to ask if you have a friend in French class, and truly that's not the most useful phrase." He smiled at the thought of some long forgotten memory.

Tucker saw his stance ease and his clenched fists ease into a more natural position.

"The three of us were friends. Our junior year, Mellie and Jason started dating. But them becoming a couple didn't cut me out. It was always the three of us. And when things got rougher my senior year, I moved in with the Matthews. Jason shared his parents with me. You don't know..." His voice cracked and he paused.

"I don't know, but I'm here, willing to listen when you're ready to tell me about Mellie and Jason, or about how you went to jail. I'm here." She took his hand. "And as for those butt-munches in there, you're better than all of them."

"I can't talk anymore."

"Yeah, I get that, too. So, come on, we're going back in. You've got friends. You're not alone."

"Angel, you don't understand."

"But I will someday. It doesn't have to be today. Unless you want to tell me more?"

He shook his head.

"Then I'll wait. For now. Come on."

As they started back into the funeral home, Bart came across the parking lot. "Sorry, Tyler. I'd've been here sooner, but my ride from school had detention and I had to scramble to find someone else who'd drive me into Erie."

Tucker put her arm around her son. "Come on, let's get Tyler back into his family. They're going to need him."

She led him back into the funeral home, and glared at all the people who parted for them. She glanced at her father and the guys from the shop and she knew if something happened to her, they'd be the first ones there to support her. If she was accused of a crime, they wouldn't believe it. And if she told them she'd done it, they'd be the first ones trying to defend her.

She walked past her dad and friends, past the line of people to the front where Jason's mother and father stood. Jace spotted her and squirmed to get down, then toddled his way like a drunken sailor in her direction. "Hey, munchkin," she murmured, scooping him up.

"Tyler. There you are," Mrs. Matthews said. "Come stand with us. You know most of Jason's friends. We don't."

"Mr. and Mrs. Matthews, I'm Tucker. A friend of Tyler's. I never had a chance to meet your son, but knowing who he chose to spend his time with, well, I have no doubt that not knowing him is my loss. I'm so sorry for your loss."

"Oh, you're the woman who kept Jace for us. I don't know how to thank you, dear. Tyler said he was taken care of, and knowing that—not having to worry about him—was a comfort. Thank you." The grey-haired woman swept Tucker into a hug. "We're lucky our Tyler has a friend like you."

Tucker didn't know what to do or say, so she settled for, "Why don't I take Jace with me and let Tyler look after you for a while."

Mrs. Matthews eyed her grandson who was happily plucking at Tucker's hair, playing with the curls.

"Thank you."

Mr. Matthews extended his hand, and shook hers, repeating his wife's words.

With the baby in her arms, she sidestepped the grieving family and moved in front of the casket. This was Jason Matthews. Tyler's friend. Jace's father. She'd never met the man, but she felt a wave of sadness at his passing. He was loved. That was as good a legacy as anyone could leave. He was loved and he was missed.

She bowed her head, offered a prayer for this man who'd been such a good friend to Tyler, then took the baby to the back of the room. Jace squirmed, indicating he wanted down, and the second his foot touched the ground, he made a beeline back through the crowd to her father, Bart and the guys from the shop. He babbled and giggled, and was quickly picked up and passed from one man to another.

Tucker watched the scene and realized she was tearing up, which was ridiculous. But she looked over at Tyler. Mrs. Matthews was standing between him and her husband, one arm around each man, clinging to them as if they were a lifeline. Tyler stood stoic at her side as one after another, people approached and paid their condolences to Jason's parents and practically ignored the fact Tyler was even there. He seemed to accept their reactions as his due, which bothered her even more.

And that's when she did cry. She blinked furiously to hold back the tears, but one escaped anyway, and she brushed it from her cheek.

TYLER DIDN'T KNOW HOW he was going to repay Angelina. She'd stayed at the funeral home all evening, supposedly to help with Jace, while in reality he was pretty sure she was watching out for him.

At least half a dozen times she appeared at his side like some tiny watchdog and took his hand, smiling at people who used to be his friends and forcing them to acknowledge he existed. He'd have preferred living in anonymity, but her staunch defense was so genuinely offered, he couldn't say anything.

So, when she'd say, "Oh, did you work with Tyler and Jason? It's very kind of you to come out to pay your respects to Jason, and show your support of Tyler. Losing a friend is hard," he'd accept his former colleague's handshake and condolences.

She'd taken the baby home with her, and left him to get Jason's parents home. He drove them back to Jason's house, where they were staying.

"Tyler, could you come in for a few minutes? I'd like to talk to you?"

"Sure, Mr. Matthews."

They went inside the small brick house that still bore Mellie's touch in every nook and cranny. Tyler had hung the rustic chandelier in the entryway with Jason. He smiled as he remembered Mellie calling out instructions about how long to make the chain it hung from. He'd helped them paint the whole house. He'd referred to the burnt orange color in the study as poop colored, but Mellie had told him he'd love it when it was done, and truth was, he did. It gave the office that Mr. Matthews led him into after he'd sent Mrs. Matthews up to bed a warm feeling.

Warmth.

That's what Mellie had brought to the house. Now, with both her and Jason gone, it felt hollow.

"I need to talk to you about what happens after the funeral tomorrow."

"You know, whatever I can do..." Tyler started.

Mr. Matthews nodded. "I do. Jason told us what you did for him, and why. I don't know what to say, Tyler."

Tyler knew that Mr. Matthews was talking about more than Tyler helping with Jace and his stomach clenched. "He shouldn't have told you."

"He wanted us to know before he went to the district attorney and confessed. I don't know why Jason didn't come to us—"

"Or me," Tyler said. "I'd have sold everything..."

"Us, too. He told me he knew that, but Mellie didn't have the time it would take to liquidate assets. He needed to get her into the experimental treatment right away and thought he had time to pay back the account before anyone noticed. He'd have never let you take the fall if Mellie hadn't been so sick."

Tyler felt sick that Jason's parents knew. He never planned to tell them, or anyone.

"Mr. Matthews, I don't want you to think Jason simply *let* me confess. When the company thought it was me, I took the blame so they wouldn't investigate further. He wanted to admit it right then, but I told him that would be selfish. Mellie needed him." Tyler choked up, remembering how hard he'd fought to keep Jason from going to the cops immediately. "He's gone now, so that's over. And I'm not sorry that no one will ever know he did it. I want Jace to grow up with a name to be proud of. Jason would never have borrowed that money if he wasn't so desperate to save Mellie. Hell, if he'd asked me, I'd have embezzled the money for him," Tyler assured Jason's father, hoping to put his guilty expression to rest.

"No, you wouldn't have," Mr. Matthews said. "You'd have found some other way, but you wouldn't have embezzled the money. And I have to believe that Jason wouldn't have done so either if he'd been thinking straight. When he started thinking clearly, he did the right thing and I support that decision. It can't negate what you went through for him, but it was a step in making it right."

"Mr. Matthews, like I said, Jason wanted to confess as soon as the company realized the money was missing. I talked him out of it. I made him let me take the fall. It was clear Mellie wouldn't have long and he needed to be there with her and with Jace."

They'd diagnosed Mellie's cancer while she was still pregnant. The doctors told her it was aggressive, that she should abort the pregnancy they'd worked so hard to achieve and begin treatment immediately, but she'd refused. She'd called her baby a miracle, and she held out hope for a second miracle. After the baby was born, her second miracle never materialized. It was too late for Mellie.

Tyler couldn't allow Jason to confess to the crime and go through the legalities and ultimately prison, if not for Jason's sake, for Mellie's. And for Jace. He didn't want his godson growing up embarrassed by his father. He wanted Jace to know he was Jason Emerich Matthews, Jr. and that was something to be proud of.

"I understand why my son did what he did. I understand his desperation. But we both know, he had other options. What you did..." Jason's father's voice broke.

He was quiet a moment as he pulled himself together then said, "It seems so unfair to ask more of you, but Tyler, we can't take Jace. Marge is finally getting back on her feet after the first hip replacement and they're starting to talk about the second surgery. I know she thinks we can, but we can't. My son had been working to clear your name, and he wrote a new will to ensure that if he hadn't managed to pay you back the money you were fined, his estate would. While he was drawing up all those legal papers, he wrote a new will and named you the baby's guardian."

Tyler had thought Mr. Matthews had asked him in to talk about the funeral tomorrow, or maybe packing up Jason's house and selling it, but not this. Not taking Jace permanently. "I can't take Jace, Mr. Matthews."

"I don't have any right to ask you. You've already done so much for our family. But we can't handle him. We were almost forty when we had Jason. We'd long since given up trying to have kids. Then he came along, a gift. We were old to be raising a child, but we were thrilled.

And though he was an only child, he brought you home and we had two sons. I love Jace, so does Marge, but we're too old to be the parents that he needs. I know Jason had no right to expect you to raise his son, that we have no right to ask you, but we can't do it and there's no one else in the world that we'd trust with our grandson."

"I never planned on having kids. You know how I grew up. They say that kind of thing is cyclical. I don't want to perpetuate—"

"Tyler, I know what your father was like, but I also know that you are not your father. I know that from the first time you came into our house, you came into our hearts, and though you're not our son by blood, we've never thought of you as anything but. So, you tell me you can't raise a baby, I'll accept it, but if you tell me the only thing standing between you and parenthood is your father, I won't."

"But you know—"

"I know that my grandson couldn't ask for a better man to take care of him. That's what I know. I know that my son couldn't have chosen a better man to call friend and brother. That's what I know. And I know that my wife and I are lucky to have you in our lives. We lost Jason, but you are still here. We still have a son. That is what I know. And lastly, I know that no matter how much Marge and I love Jace, we are not the parents he needs. We're old and she's been sick. I have no right to ask you, to expect you to throw your life into upheaval again for us, but I'm asking. Will you take Jace?"

"I will." Tyler said the words before he could think. He'd loved Jace since the moment he was born. He'd wanted to play surrogate uncle. Though the notion of playing surrogate father had never crossed his mind. He'd never considered being a parent to anyone.

He had no role model.

But as he looked at Mr. Matthews, he realized that was a lie.

He took the older man's hand in his. "I swear, I will work myself to the bone to provide for him. As long as I have a breath in me, he will never know anything but love."

Mr. Matthews clasped Tyler's hand. "I never expected anything less from you, Tyler."

"I should let you get some sleep. I'll pick you both up for the funeral tomorrow."

"There's one more thing. After the funeral, Jason's attorney is going to read his will. You'll find that you were named in it. With his insurance money, and the money from the house when we sell it, we can start to pay what we owe you."

"That money will be put away for Jace."

"There will be some left for that. But you will take the money and use it to restart your life. It's what my son wanted. He started the process, and I guarantee that I'll see it through. Let him have that comfort in death. He can't give you back everything you sacrificed for him and Mellie, but he can do this."

"Mr. Matthews..." Tyler didn't know what to say. He didn't have a clue. None of this was what he expected. None of this was what he wanted.

After losing Mellie, Jason should have suffered enough. Now he was gone. And the life Tyler thought he'd have was gone as well.

He was going to raise Jace.

Images of his father played in his head, like some never-ending slide show. The words he'd hurled like fists when he wasn't using his actual fists. All of it.

What if Mr. Matthews was wrong? What if Tyler was doomed to repeat his father's mistakes?

There was no easy answer.

All he could do was his best.

He thought of Angelina and something in him eased. She'd been little more than a child herself when she'd had Bart, and she'd done a hell of a job with the boy. She would never let anything happen to Jace. If he asked, she'd check on him and make sure he never slipped up.

It was a lot to ask of someone who'd already given him a job when no one else would. Someone who believed in him without ever asking for explanations. Someone who stood by him when old friends turned their backs on him.

Instinctually he knew that Angelina Tucker would agree.

She was a tiny woman, but she had a warrior's heart.

She'd never let him hurt Jace.

If he fell into his past, she'd save the baby.

He knew that, and that knowledge allowed him to hope he could succeed at this.

CHAPTER FOUR

THE FRIDAY AFTER JASON'S funeral, Tucker asked herself for about the thousandth time what she was doing. The answer remained the same—she didn't have a clue. But not knowing what she was doing didn't stop her from pulling into the driveway of an old farmhouse. The cedar siding had once been white, but had worn until it was grey and weathered.

The porch was huge, but also weathered. Two old rockers sat on either side of a small wooden table with a huge fern.

When she'd thought about where Tyler lived, she'd pictured a condo where everything was white and black, sleek and chrome. Something out of a magazine.

Not this.

She hadn't seen him since the funeral service. She'd gone with all the guys from the shop and Bart. They'd sat in the back of the church while Tyler sat up front with Jason's parents.

Even with the length of a church separating them, Tyler's sadness was palpable. She understood that kind of friendship. That's what her relationship with Eli was—closer than sisters. She had other friends, but there was a special bond with Eli. The thought of losing her friend was enough to make her knees buckle. It didn't take any stretch of her imagination to know how hard losing his friend had hit Tyler.

And that's what she was doing here on his porch. She somehow wanted to ease that pain for him. Before talking herself out of it, Tucker knocked on the door.

Moments later, Tyler opened it, Jace on his shoulder. Jace whimpered. It was the kind of sound that said he was getting over a fussy jag.

"Hi, munchkin. I thought you'd be on your way to Florida by now," she said. "What's got you all upset?"

"I told him no," Tyler said, sounding as upset as Jace. "He was reaching for the stove, and I said no, but I think I must have said it too harshly because he started this."

"Kids don't like hearing *no*, babies, toddlers or teens—doesn't matter. They want their own way. Being sharp when he tried to touch the stove was a good thing. He could hear in your voice that it's totally off-limits. There's no negotiation on the issue. Be consistent. When you say no, mean no. If he gets upset, do what you're doing—comfort him. Comfort but don't give in."

"You think it's okay to comfort him after I was the one who upset him?" Tyler asked.

"Sure. When you're upset, even if it's because of something you did, don't you want someone to comfort you?"

"No," came his flat response.

Tucker realized she'd put her foot in it. She thought about the way his ex-colleagues had acted at the funeral home. She felt even more sympathy for him. She held the baking dish out. "I brought a lasagne. I'll put it in your fridge, if you point the way."

"You didn't have to do that."

"Well, I know the guys would have sent something, too, but it wouldn't have been safe to eat. Not one of them can do much more than peanut butter and jelly sandwiches. North ran out of jelly once and made a peanut butter and dry Jello sandwich. Of course, he has less taste than the rest of them. He puts peanut butter and mustard on his hot dogs." She was babbling and knew it, but didn't know how to stop. There was the fact of Tyler kissing her standing between them. Her babbling helped bridge that fact; at least for her it did. "I don't know why people bring food when someone suffers a loss, but they do, so I'm here."

"Thanks."

She put the lasagne in the refrigerator and couldn't help but notice it wasn't filled with other offerings of food from friends. She wanted to do something more for Tyler, but couldn't think of what.

"You'll have to heat it up when you want it. And there's enough to last a couple days, or it freezes well."

She looked around the kitchen. It was old enough to be almost retro-chic. There were floor to ceiling cabinets, a giant country sink and old white enamel appliances. Again, it's not the sort of kitchen she'd pictured Tyler having.

Tyler Martinez was an enigma.

"Seems like he's calmed down," she said.

"Yeah." Tyler put Jace on the floor and the baby toddled over to Tucker. She knelt down and said, "How're you doing, munchkin?"

Jace babbled some response, then walked toward the stove and said, very clearly, "No."

Tucker smiled. "Good boy, that's a no."

"No, no, no, no." Jace waggled his chubby finger at the stove, but didn't get too close or touch it.

Tucker glanced up at Tyler and smiled. "See, I think you made your point."

"But I made him cry."

"There's no reasoning with babies. Actually, he's more of a toddler." She remembered when she accepted Bart wasn't a baby anymore. The feeling of nostalgia engulfed her. He was a high school graduate as of yesterday. Legally an adult.

She'd sat with Pops, Eli, her husband Zac and the guys from the shop. All of them had helped raise him. All of them reveled in the moment he took his diploma and moved the tassel of his cap from one side to the other.

80

Her son was a graduate.

She felt adrift for a moment. And at the end of the summer, he'd be gone. She'd spent her entire adult life as Bart's mom. She was still his mom, but it wasn't the same.

Jace walked his drunken-sailor walk over to some wood blocks and plopped onto the floor.

"Yeah," Tyler agreed. "I guess toddling has to be the definition of toddler."

They stood in companionable silence for a minute that went from comfortable to awkward for Tucker. Time to go. She'd done her duty and brought him lasagne. "So we'll see you at the shop on Monday."

"About that?" Tyler said.

"Yes?"

"Jace has a regular sitter in Erie, but she's out of town, and I have to find someone closer anyway, but I haven't had time to interview anyone. I—"

"Wait a minute." The impact of what he was saying sank in. "You're keeping the baby?"

He nodded. "I didn't plan on it, but the Matthews are getting older and Mrs. Matthews had one hip replaced and they need to do the other one. They love him, love being his grandparents, but can't play surrogate parents. Jason was an only child, so there's not one else on that side, and Mellie didn't have any immediate family. That leaves me. Jason named me Jace's guardian in his will. I tried to convince his dad they could find someone better to raise him. He wouldn't listen."

"I'm glad he didn't, because I don't believe that they could have found anyone better," Tucker said. She had to admit that on the surface an ex-con as a guardian for a young child seemed less than ideal. But watching Tyler with the baby, it was evident that he loved him and would do his best for him. A kid couldn't ask for more than that.

"I didn't plan on having kids...ever. I have no idea what I'm doing."

Rather than beating a hasty escape, Tucker sat down at one of the kitchen chairs and Tyler followed suit.

Jace occasionally looked up from his pile of blocks and no-noed the stove.

"Listen, Ty, I understand feeling overwhelmed and I understand that given your...past, this is especially hard. Well, my situation was especially hard, too. I didn't plan on being a parent, especially not when I was still in high school, but there it was. I had a teacher in my corner. Eli found programs and opportunities in the community for me. Hell, she started the whole teen parenting program because she found the system was lacking when she tried to help me. Even after I graduated, she went from teacher to friend. And Pops was great, once he got over the initial shock, but mainly it was me and Bart."

"What about Bart's father?"

After all these years, Tucker rarely thought about Bart's father. She didn't blame him for walking away, but she did feel bad for him. He should have been sitting with them yesterday marveling in how amazing his son was. "He's never had anything to do with Bart. What I'm saying is, I didn't plan it. I had good people in my corner to help when I needed it, but so do you." He looked confused.

Tucker didn't feel insulted, she simply got specific. "You've got me, Pops and the guys at work. And we need you back at the garage, so bring Jace to me Monday morning."

"Tucker, I couldn't."

"You can and will. Bart's working as a lifeguard at the Sunrise Foundation's day camp this summer, three days a week, so he'll be around a few days to help, and I'll stick some toys in the front office and that portable crib. Jace can hang with me while I do the dreaded paperwork each day."

"What about your painting?"

"I can do that after hours, or schedule it so I can do it on Bart's days off. And Pops is around. Odds are he's going to grumble, but he loves kids. He'll help. This isn't the first time Tucker's Garage has dealt with a baby. North and Joe weren't around when Bart was little, but it was nothing to see Lou holding my son as he talked to a customer, or Pops talking softly on the phone in his office because Bart was taking a nap. We'll make it work. Come in on Monday and bring a diaper bag."

"Tucker, I couldn't—"

"You can. You work for Tucker's Garage. It's okay to need and accept help, Tyler," she added. "When I had Bart, everyone pitched in and I never felt as if I was doing it alone. You're not going to either."

"But—"

Tucker knew that laying down the law was sometimes the easiest thing to do. "I'm the boss, so there's no butting. Bring him in on Monday."

He cracked the ghost of a smile. "You're trying to sound scary, but it doesn't work."

Tucker sighed. "Yeah, that's not the first time I've been told I'm not scary. But be that as it may, bring him. You'll find someone permanently soon enough, but until then, we can make it work."

Tucker saw that he was going to protest some more. "Hey, I'm not looking for a permanent babysitting career. Been there, done that and as soon as Bart heads to college this fall, I'm done. I'm planning to start living my life for me."

"What plans?"

Tucker felt relieved that he was smiling. "Big plans." She tried to think of something she'd do when Bart was gone...something different. "Maybe a cruise?"

Tyler chuckled. "Yeah, you're wild."

She shrugged. "I don't really know how to live a life where all I have to worry about is me. But I'll figure it out. And you'll figure out how to handle Jace."

"We're sort of living life in opposite directions."

"We've always had that opposite...uh, thing going for us." She'd almost said opposites attract, but had managed a nice save.

Tyler nodded, as if he understood what she was saying, which was great because Tucker wasn't entirely sure herself.

Tyler still looked confused. "I don't know how to thank you."

Tucker stood. "You don't have to try and thank us. It comes with the job description." She pushed her chair back under the table. "So, I'll see you both on Monday, bright and early."

He nodded. "Fine. We'll be there."

She made a dash for the front door before he could change his mind, or start arguing again.

"Hey, Tucker," Tyler said, the baby on his hip as he followed her.

Damn. She'd almost made a clean break. She kept her hand on the doorknob as she turned. "Yes?"

"I have never claimed to understand women, but I've decided you're more mystifying than most. I was under the impression you didn't like me, so I'm not sure why you've gone out of your way for me, but I appreciate it."

His statement surprised her. "I never disliked you, Tyler. I thought we covered this before—I was put out that Pops had hired you without consulting me. And of course, he'd just told me he was retiring. You know that phrase, *it isn't you, it's me?* That applies here. I didn't not like you, it was simply a lot to process."

"It wasn't only that first day at work," he said with a shrug. "You always said no when I asked you out."

"Well, I've told a lot of guys no—doesn't mean I disliked them, only that I didn't think we'd suit each other. Suits." She remembered joking with Eli over being asked out by a guy who would always be better dressed than she was. "That was part of it. We're just so different. I couldn't see the point in us dating. That doesn't mean I didn't like you."

Tyler didn't look convinced. "Oh." He paused a moment, as if he'd been processing her words, then asked, "So if I'd been wearing jeans instead of a designer suit when I asked you out, you'd have said yes?"

"It was what it was.... I don't play what-if games."

"But what if?" he pressed.

Tucker shook her head. "Still not going to play. I gave up on what-ifs when I had Bart—he didn't need a playmate, he needed a mother, so I grew up. I don't deal in the hypothetical, but rather in what is. I became a woman who works

86

in a man's world. I grew up," she repeated. "And grown-ups don't play what-if games."

Tyler stared at her chest. He didn't seem the kind of guy to stare at a woman's breasts, so she spotted what he was looking at. Her T-shirt was a girly pink and had pictures of battered butterflies and read *How Could You Tell I Ride a Motorcycle*?

"I don't know that you grew up all the way," Tyler pointed out.

Tucker shrugged, but felt her cheeks flame. "I didn't buy the shirt. A customer gave it to me."

Tyler nodded, his expression serious. "It looks a bit playful to me. Almost as if the person wearing it has a bit of an inner-child left."

"It doesn't look playful. It looks tough. Those butterflies are smooshed."

"They're still butterflies. And it's pink. Very pink. That says playful and girly."

"I still don't play what-ifs," she maintained.

Tyler smiled. "Thanks. That's the first laugh I've had in...well, in a while."

Tucker tried to look stern, but it was hard. She was relieved to see Tyler loosening up. "You're nuts. I'm a hard ass, and you probably should realize that."

"Tucker, you can pretend you're tough, but it's all a facade. In addition to being a sweet woman who likes to wear pink, you're a pushover. And you're a good friend."

"Sweet?" Tucker scoffed as she finally opened the door and beat a hasty retreat. Sweet? No one had called her sweet...ever.

She glanced back over her shoulder at Tyler. He was still laughing. Well, if thinking she was sweet lightened his load a bit, then so be it. His misperception was a small price to pay to pick him up a bit.

But Monday, she was definitely not going to wear a pink t-shirt.

She had tons of black t-shirts. She'd wear one of those.

Black and tough looking.

Tyler wouldn't be thinking she was sweet on Monday.

She stopped huffing and thought about Tyler and the baby. She'd found herself a parent at an unexpected moment in her life.

Now he was going through the same thing.

Wanting to help him didn't mean she was sweet. It simply meant she understood better than most people could.

TYLER SOMEHOW MANAGED to get out of the house on time Monday morning, but it was a near thing. Getting Jace up, dressed, fed and out the door was tough. He was thankful he'd packed the diaper bag Sunday night.

He still didn't feel right allowing Angelina to throw her day into chaos in order to help him, but he needed this job. He'd put in a call to an agency, hoping to find a sitter, but he didn't expect to hear anything right away. He could check out daycare centers, but he'd prefer the baby have one-on-one care. For now, Jace at work with Tucker's help was his best option. His only option.

Once Jace's regular sitter was home, he could always see if she'd keep watching Jace, though that would mean a half-hour commute to get him to Pam's in the morning, and then another half hour back to Whedon in time for work. Not a great situation, but for now, it was all he had.

He entered the shop. No one was in the garage, so he walked back to Angelina's office and knocked.

"Come in."

He went in and burst out laughing. Angelina was wearing a black t-shirt with a skull and crossbones on it, under which it read *Biker—'Nuf Said.*

"Do you even ride motorcycles?" he managed to ask.

"Of course, I can ride them. I simply don't often, and I've never owned one. I do paint them, and the guys I do work for have noticed my t-shirt collection and feed my habit."

He knew the black shirt was in response to his teasing about the pink one and couldn't resist assuring her that "Skulls don't make you look tougher. You're a marshmallow. And if I've noticed that after only a few weeks of being here, odds are everyone else knows it, too."

Her insistence that he let her help with Jace cemented her marshmallow status in his mind. They were traveling in opposite directions—her son was leaving home, and he suddenly had a baby—yet, marshmallow that she was, she'd put her almost-childless status on hold to help him out. He couldn't help wondering what might have happened if she'd said yes when he'd originally asked her out. It was probably for the best that she hadn't accepted. Because if they'd gotten together, when he fell into the mud, Angelina, being Angelina, would have jumped in, too. She was entitled to more than that. More than him.

"Marshmallow?" she repeated. "If I dock your pay for calling me names, you'll see that I'm no marshmallow." She couldn't even convince herself she was that tough. "Fine. You've discovered my deep, dark secret. Now, hand over the baby and get to work. There, did that sound tough enough to you?"

"No, but it will have to do." He passed Jace into her open arms and put the diaper bag down. "Thanks, Angelina—"

"It's Tucker, use it on a regular basis like everyone else does."

"Your name is rather like that t-shirt. You think being a Tucker rather than an Angelina makes you seem tougher, but you're wrong. At your core, you're Angelina and I can see that, even if everyone else you work with can't."

She scowled, but even that wasn't overly convincing. He quirked his eyebrow and grinned.

Angelina sighed. "Get to work, or I'm seriously going to dock you. Me and Jace have some invoices to go over."

He leaned down and kissed Jace's forehead. Every fiber of his being yearned to do the same to Angelina. A simple soft, sweet kiss on the forehead to start his day on the right note, but he suspected it wouldn't start hers on anything close to a right note, so he resisted.

He'd wanted her for a long time, despite the fact she'd consistently turned him down. He still wanted her, but what could he really offer her now? So he simply waved goodbye and left them to get reacquainted.

He checked on Lou's manifest and started repairing a beautiful 1956 Ford F100 truck. There were flames bursting from the headlights back to the truck's tailgate. The letters AT were worked seamlessly into the bottom right of the design. Angelina Tucker.

She was a gifted artist.

A businesswoman.

A mother.

And a hell of a friend.

He wouldn't push her for more than she wanted to give. That didn't stop him for wishing things were different. That when he'd asked her out before he'd kept trying, even after she'd said no repeatedly.

Mrs. Matthews used to say, if wishes were horses beggars would ride. But when Jason's family had taken him in and made him one of them, he'd discovered that sometimes wishes came true. He simply had to remember that because it happened once, didn't mean it would happen again. Lightning only struck once.

Before he could begin, Lou and Mr. Tucker came in.

"Good to see you back." Lou sounded genuinely pleased to see him. "We've got a lot on at the moment."

"Can I talk to you before you start working?" Mr. Tucker asked.

"Sure." He followed Angelina's father outside.

George Tucker had always seemed a bit larger than life. But he seemed smaller these days. It wasn't the diet Angelina had, according to sources, put him on, it was the fact he'd been ill. He suddenly looked his age. Balding, white haired and less robust. He still maintained an air of joviality, that was now replaced by seriousness. "I wanted to tell you again how sorry I am for your loss."

"Thank you, sir."

"Angel tells me she volunteered to help with the baby," he said slowly, studying Tyler with an uncomfortable intensity as he said the words.

Tyler nodded. "Yes, but I don't want you to think I'm going to take advantage of her offer. I'm looking for a sitter already and—"

"That's not what I was going to say, Tyler. I was going to say, thank you. Angel, she needs to realize there's more to life than the business. In the past, she's had Bart to balance her out, but he'll be gone in a few months, and maybe spending time with the baby will remind her there's a lot out there for her, if she'll only go for it. I've been trying to talk her into letting me sell my share of the business to someone. A partner would allow her to have more time for a life. I'm hoping Jace will help me convince her of that."

"Sir, I know I don't know your daughter that well, but it seems to me, if Angelina wanted something, she'd go after it."

"Oh, you're right, but the thing is, she's never known anything other than working at the shop and hanging out with us. There might be more that she wants, only she doesn't have enough experience to recognize it."

"I see your point." Still, Tyler believed that if Angelina felt shorted, she'd go out and rectify that.

"I talked to the guys," Mr. Tucker continued, "and we'll all pitch in until you can work out something else for the baby."

"Thank you, sir." Tyler didn't know what else to say. "I mean it, thank you. For everything. For the job in the first place, for letting me take last week off, for the help. Just thanks." There was nothing more to say after that. He headed back to the Ford.

George Tucker called, "One more thing," and stopped him in his tracks.

"I've seen how you look at my daughter."

Tyler immediately started to argue. "I—"

Mr. Tucker cut him off. "There's no use denying it."

Before Tyler could come up with a response, George Tucker clapped a hand on his shoulder. "I like you, son. Always did, and it had nothing to do with the expensive cars you drove and the business you threw our way. I liked you. That hasn't changed. I believe in second chances, but I also believe my daughter deserves more than someone who's had trouble with the law. Do I make myself clear?"

Tyler nodded. "Crystal."

"Fine. Now, I'm going to see if Tucker will loan me Jace for a bit. We're going to pull some weeds in my garden. It's shady enough this time of the morning, he won't get burned."

"Thank you, sir."

They went inside and Tyler watched Angelina's father stroll toward her office.

He totally understood Mr. Tucker's concern. The man had been good to him, offering him a job when no one else would. Pitching in to help with Jace until he could get things settled.

But more than a good friend, he was a great father who only wanted the best for his daughter. Some men might take offense at his concern, but Tyler didn't. He wanted the best for Angelina, too. And he, better than anyone else, knew that wasn't him.

For a while he'd thought he'd overcome his past, but here he was, exactly where his father had been—an ex-con who worked in a garage with a kid who was relying on him.

Oh, he didn't drink like his father, but otherwise he'd have to be blind not to see the similarities.

Angelina deserved more than he could ever give her.

So, he'd accept her help for his godson's sake, but he'd look hard and fast for another alternative.

Angelina had been thrust into adulthood when she was little more than a child herself. When Bart went to college in the fall, she'd finally have the opportunity to live for herself. To be independent.

He wanted that for her.

That and so much more.

Tyler went to work on the truck, and tried to put thoughts of kissing Angelina out of his mind.

He didn't need her father to warn him off.

He'd see to that himself.

"Hey, Pops. You two done in the garden?" Tucker asked a few hours later as her father came into her office.

"We got most of the weeding done. Jace finds worms highly entertaining, and slightly edible."

She must have looked upset because he hurried to assure her, "Don't worry. I didn't let him eat it. But it was a near thing."

"I'm pretty sure Bart ate a few things I'd find less than palatable, so I'll try not to sweat it. But maybe we should get you something better to snack on?" she asked Jace as she took him into her arms, then turned back to her father. "I got finished the Burhenn's paint job on that Jeep. It's the first time someone asked me to airbrush a Jeep."

"When you're good, you're good. Doesn't matter what your canvas is."

"Thanks. I'm going to try to get Jace down for a nap, then make some calls. The guys all said they'd stagger their lunches, so he can play with them and I can go back to the paint room."

"Sounds like you've got it all under control."

"I think so. Bart's home at three and said he'll get him then."

"It takes me back to when we were all juggling him," her father said. "Hard to believe he's graduated now."

"Yes, it's hard to believe," Tucker murmured and handed Jace a sippy cup of milk, followed by a handful of Cheerios. They read Russell Hoban's *Bread and Jam for Frances* together, and within minutes, he was down for the count.

She tucked the baby into the porta-crib, turned on her iPod in its dock in order to provide some background noise, then returned to her desk.

Maybe she should consider her father's suggestion that she take on a partner. If she kept controlling shares, and had someone else to do the books, it might not be too bad. She could hire someone to do them without letting go of any of the business, but she wouldn't for the same reason her father never had—it was tough to trust someone who didn't have a vested interest in a company.

Bart was off to college as an undeclared major, but had talked about doing something with business, or numbers.

Maybe he'd get his MBA? A degree in accounting?

She sighed. That was years down the line, and odds are he wouldn't want to work in the shop. As much as she might fantasize about having a partner who didn't mind paperwork, odds are she'd never give up any control in the company. No partners for her.

Paperwork was in her future.

She sighed again and scanned her call-back list. She'd started dialing the first number when Eli appeared in the doorway. Eli Cartwright Keller had been the teacher who'd helped Tucker so much when she'd found out she was pregnant. Three years ago, Eli had found unexpectedly pregnant. Even though Eli had been long-past teenhood, she'd gone through a lot. The baby's father had deserted her, which gave Zac Keller the chance he'd been waiting for. He was raising her son as his own, and they'd adopted a little girl together.

"Shh," Tucker warned her friend, and pointed to the baby sleeping in the crib.

"Something you want to tell me?" Eli asked softly, sinking into the chair across from Tucker and nodding her head at the baby. "I know I've been caught up in the end of school year chaos, but...?"

Tucker wasn't sure where to start. Hell, she wasn't sure why she hadn't called Eli and filled her in on the whole situation earlier. "Remember that guy who kept asking me out a few years ago?"

"A lot of guys ask you out, Tuck."

"Yeah, this was the one I wouldn't go out with. Mr. Designer Suits?"

Eli laughed. "Oh, him I do remember."

Tyler had been pestering her for a date at the same time Zac was trying to win Eli over. Zac had succeeded, Tyler hadn't. "Well, Tyler works for us now and..." She launched into the story.

Eli studied Jace a moment. "So, you're helping him out with the baby?"

"Yes."

"And he kissed you and you kissed him back?"

"Only once, and only a little. I don't think it meant anything," Tucker justified. "He was upset and needed comfort."

"And you?"

"Huh?"

"He was upset, and I get that. People want to feel connected to someone else when something horrible happens to them. He reached out to you. That explains him kissing you. But you kissing him?"

Tucker started and sputtered to aborted explanations for a moment, then finally settled on, "I...I was only being nice."

Eli burst out laughing. "You can tell yourself that all you want, but I'm not buying it."

"You're saying I'm not nice?"

"I'm saying that in all the years I've known you, you have always been nice, but that kindness didn't include kissing for comfort. Name one other man you've ever kissed out of mere compassion because they were traumatized?"

Tucker didn't know what to say to that. She didn't even know why she'd mentioned that barely mentionable kiss to Eli and deeply regretted that she had. Eli was going to blow it all out of proportion.

"So, what's standing in your way now?" Eli asked. "If he's working here, he must have retired the fancy outfits, right?"

"His life's in turmoil. He's barely got out of jail, lost a friend and inherited a baby. That is not a good candidate for dating."

"And you?" Eli pressed.

Tucker blustered, "What about me?" She knew she sounded defensive. Too defensive.

Eli Keller had fallen head-over-heals in love a few years ago, and now was terminally afflicted with fantasies of happily-ever-afters.

"What about you?" Eli repeated. "It's all him and his problems standing in the way of you dating him, hmm?"

"Sure it's him. I don't have any problems."

Eli's teasing evaporated, and she looked serious. "Tucker, we've been friends for years. I've watched you with men—"

"Hey, don't say it like that. You make it sound like I've had a long line of men."

"No, that might not be as troublesome as the fact that the few guys you go out with are men you'd never seriously consider anything long term with."

"I've dated some very nice men."

Eli nodded. "You did. But you didn't find any of them nice enough for more than a few dates."

"I practice a catch and release system of dating." She'd explained that philosophy to Eli in the past and they'd laughed, but Eli wasn't laughing now, so she added, "I like my independence."

"I think it's more than that. Bart's father did a number on you."

No way was Tucker using that lame crutch. "Eli, that was years ago. I was a kid, and so was he. I certainly don't believe I can never find love because one teenage fling didn't work out. Give me some credit."

"Then what is it?" Eli asked. "I've never figured it out."

Tucker sighed, not sure she had either. "I know when Bart was little, I worried about bringing a guy into the mix. You hear horror stories about men who resent raising other people's sons."

"Zac didn't, doesn't, resent raising Johnny."

Tucker had seen Eli husband with their son, and there was no doubt in her mind that Zac thought of Johnny as his own. "I know. I said, when Bart was little. I eventually figured out that I was strong enough to protect him if need be, but that odds are, any guy I fell for wouldn't require it. So, that's not it. Maybe once, but not any more. I date. And I like to think I open myself up to the idea of each man's potential. The problem is, I've never met a guy I wanted to spend more than a few dates with. I want..."

"What?" Eli asked. "What are you looking for in a guy?"

"I want a partner. Someone I can relate to. Someone who accepts me for who I am, not who they want me to be. Let's face it, I'm not the traditional woman. I'll never spend my time cooking gourmet meals, or ironing some guy's underwear. I need him to being willing to accept that I'm happiest in the garage with grease under my fingernails, and paint smudged...everywhere. When I find that in a man, I'll snag him." She made an X over her chest. "Cross my heart."

Eli sighed. "Okay, that will have to do."

Tucker laughed. "I'm glad you think so. And while I love it when you visit, I suspect you didn't come see me to harangue me about men, or my lack thereof."

"No, the haranguing was spontaneous," she said with a laugh. "I actually came over to invite you to a Hurrah-the-School-Year's-Over Party, otherwise known as a Keller excuse to get together at my house."

"And by invite, you mean attendance is mandatory." Since Eli married into the Keller family, Tucker had been to more than a few Keller parties; she knew the score.

"Now, Tucker, you know I'd never say that. Mrs. Keller, she might say it. Okay, so she often says it. You can be sure she'll expect you, your dad and Bart there."

"Every time I show up at a Keller function, the official and unofficial family has grown."

"Kellerized," they both said in unison. Years ago, when Mr. and Mrs. Keller discovered they couldn't have children, they'd adopted six, including Eli's husband, Zac. Over the years, they'd continued to add to the family without any more formal adoptions. When Eli married Zac, Tucker got Kellerized through osmosis, then her father and Bart were added as well.

102

"Will Laura and Seth be there?"

Eli nodded. "With the baby."

"You had me at baby," Tucker admitted. "We'll be there."

"Why don't you bring Tyler and Jace, too," Eli offered.

"I'm not going to have you trying to set me up with him, Eli Keller."

"That hadn't occurred to me, but I'm encouraged that it occurred to you," her friend said with a grin. "I simply thought as an unexpected new parent he might like to hang around with some old pros. And goodness knows the Kellers are all pros."

Tucker felt stupid. "Oh."

"Yeah, oh."

Eli grinned so broadly, Tucker feared her face would crack. "Wipe that smile off your face."

Tucker watched as Eli tried. Valiantly. But without success.

"Sorry," she finally said, grin firmly in place. "You're kind of cute like this."

"Like what?" Tucker asked.

"Flustered by a man."

"I am not." When Eli kept grinning, Tucker stated even more firmly, "I am not flustered by Tyler Martinez. I'm his friend. Only a friend. That's it. That's all she wrote, folks. I'm helping him out like I'd help out any of the guys that work here. I'm not looking for anything more than friendship. I'm looking forward to this next chapter of my life. Bart will go to school and for the first time in my entire adult life, the only person I'm responsible for is me. I'll be exploring what independence is really like."

Eli nodded, looking totally unbelieving. She gave Tucker the party info and said, "See you there," as she hurried out of the office.

Tucker stared at the closed door.

She meant what she'd said. She was looking forward to figuring out who she was going to be in this new phase of her life.

Solo.

She'd never used that word about herself before.

It felt odd.

And secretly she acknowledged, a little lonely.

CHAPTER FIVE

TYLER GLANCED ACROSS the car at Tucker, her words from last week played over again in his head. He'd been about to knock on her partially opened door when he'd heard her say, "for the first time in my entire adult life, the only person I'm responsible for is me. I'll be exploring what independence is really like." Who could blame her?

He'd wanted to say no to her invitation to the Keller picnic, but he'd found her argument that the Kellers were baby experts compelling. He could use all the help with Jace he could get. He knew he was ill-prepared for raising a child.

The baby was in the back, and Bart and his grandfather were coming a bit later. They'd decided to bring two cars in case Jace acted up and he needed to leave.

"Angelina, while I have you to myself," he started, and realized that hadn't come out the way he wanted it to. "I'm trading in my truck and buying a truck with a backseat, so I can return your car soon."

"Okay. It hasn't been a problem though."

He shrugged. "I don't like asking for favors."

"You didn't ask," she pointed out.

"I know. You offered. Like you offered to watch Jace. His old babysitter is back in town, and she said she'd be happy to watch him until I can arrange for someone closer."

"In Erie?" Angelina asked slowly, as if thinking about it.

He nodded.

"I don't know that I think driving into Erie and back for work, then doing it in reverse after work is the best use of your time. Jace is fine with us until you find someone closer."

When he told her that she didn't need to look after a baby any more, he expected a sigh of relief on her part, not an argument. "Angel, I'm taking advantage of you, and—"

She snorted. No dainty ladylike laugh, or some quiet attempt to dissuade him. A snort. "Yeah, because I'm wrapped so tightly around your finger, you can make me do anything—even what I don't want to do. I'm just a weak-willed woman who can be forced into things by a big strong man like you."

He knew he needed to say something, but he wasn't sure what in the face of her sarcasm. "I'm sorry. I—"

"No, I'm sorry. Sometimes my mouth slips into gear before my brain can catch up with it. It's nice that you're worried about taking advantage, but you're not," she told him. "I don't think I had Jace more than an hour or so a day. I have at least that much to do in the office for that long. Did you know I have to file all kinds of tax stuff quarterly? And let's not even talk about payroll. Checking time cards, calculating overtime. And ordering. The invoices never stop rolling in, and I think they should be paid immediately because as a small business owner, I know they all rely on their money coming in regularly, like we do. And I don't even want to think about the end of year extras."

"I take it paperwork isn't your favorite thing?"

"I'd rather clean toilets—the ones in the garage bathroom, which I won't use myself. That should tell you something."

He let out a long, low whistle. "Any time you need help, holler. I'm good with keeping books and money..." He let the sentence trail off as he remembered he was a convicted embezzler. He never thought of himself as such, but he knew the rest of the world did—and rightly so. "Sorry. That was a stupid offer."

"One I'm happy to say yes to. I'm not too proud to take help with the paperwork."

"But you shouldn't take help from me." He waved a hand in the air. "Convict, remember?"

"I've wanted to ask you about that. Why—"

He cut her off. "There's nothing to tell. They accused, I didn't argue with them, I went to jail, served my time and paid restitution."

"You sold off everything?"

He thought about Mr. Matthews saying that they wanted to pay him back from Jason's estate. He should be pleased, but he wasn't. Taking that money would seem like an admission that Jason owed him, when in reality, he owed Jason a debt he'd never be able to repay—and never could now.

He thought about how to answer Angelina. "I liquidated almost everything. The condo, the cars. I had enough left to buy the farmhouse and the truck, so, no, I'm not destitute by any stretch of the imagination. I've got a roof over my head, enough food to eat. I'm fine."

He knew what it was like to look in a cupboard and find it literally bare. He knew what it was like to start school with no supplies, no new shoes or clothes. His father hadn't paid the water bill and they'd turned it off one summer. Tyler had scraped up enough money to do his clothes at the laundromat most of the time, but a few times he couldn't even manage that. He'd had to go to his neighbor and ask to use her machines. It was one of his most humbling memories.

"I've got enough," he assured Angelina, "so I'm fine. I will always see to it Jace has what he needs." It was more a promise to himself.

"Well, back to Jace, the offer stands. Paying Jace's sitter will only be one more bill on your already stretched finances, and Tyler, I really enjoy having him around. We all do. It reminds me so much of when Bart was young."

He could hear the wistfulness in her voice.

"I—"

"We're here."

They pulled up in front of Eli's house. Rather than go to the front door, she led him around the house on a brick walkway. "The party's in back. Eli's place isn't big enough for Keller functions inside."

As they passed under a small vine covered arbor, Tyler got his first glance at the Keller family. When Angelina had issued the invite, he'd said no. He didn't want to go to a party with a bunch of strangers—strangers who more than likely knew about his past. But Angelina had told him that Mr. and Mrs. Keller had adopted their six children. Her friend Eli had adopted a daughter as well. If anyone could give him tips on parenting Jace, they could.

When she threw Jace's well-being into the equation, he didn't have any choice but to say yes. He'd do anything—even go to a party—for Jace.

"Tucker," a number of them yelled when they spotted her.

"Hey," she called back, then grabbed his hand and pulled him into the throng. "This is the garage's newest employee, my friend Tyler, and this is his godson, Jace. He's going to be raising Jace, and I told him he couldn't find any better authorities on childrearing than the Kellers. Don't make a liar out of me. Tyler this is..."

She pointed and rattled off names. He caught a number, but not all. Eli, her husband Zac Keller and their kids, Ebony and Johnny. Another Keller, Seth, and his wife Laura with their son, Jamie. There were more Kellers, and a number of people who didn't seem to be Kellers, but seemed like part of the family regardless.

When he could fade back from the throng, he did. Taking Jace with him to a quiet corner where he could study the loud, happy family.

So, this was what it was like. A real family.

He studied Abe and Deborah Keller, a large grizzled man and a tiny, round woman with salt and pepper hair and an ever-present smile. How did two people open their home and heart to six children who weren't theirs? Not only the kids they adopted, but by the looks of this party, they'd opened their hearts to half of Whedon as well.

Mr. Keller was talking to a man who Angelina had introduced as Colm. She'd told Tyler that Colm was special, and from the rapt attention Mr. Keller was giving him, he thought so, too. Mrs. Keller was chatting to a young girl with buzz cut hair, and more piercings than he'd ever seen on a kid. But it didn't seem as if Mrs. Keller saw the goth looking clothes, or the piercings. She simply listened and smiled at what the kid was saying, giving the girl her undivided attention.

He checked on Jace, who was sitting next to him on the grass, batting at a branch on the hedge.

"Penny for your thoughts."

He turned and saw Eli Keller behind him. She plopped down on the grass next to him, seemingly unconcerned about stains on her light tan shorts.

He didn't know how to respond, and before he could formulate something, she continued, "Being Kellerized can be a bit overwhelming."

"Kellerized?"

"Tucker came up with it. It's how she describes being absorbed by the family and counted as one of their own. When you're accustomed to a more solitary existence, it can be even harder to adjust to the Kellerization."

"How can you tell I lead a solitary existence?"

She laughed. "You're over here with Jace, and everyone else is over there. That was my first hint."

He smiled. "So you're a detective as well as a teacher?"

"I think that both jobs require the same sort of observation."

Jace stood and toddled over to Eli and flopped in her lap. She wrapped her arms around him, as if it were second nature. "Tucker said you're going to be raising Jace?"

"Yes." He still wasn't sure how it had happened. He wasn't even sure if it was wise.

"She told me she was going to use that as a way to lure you into our clutches." Eli chuckled. "If you have any questions, we're here. You're lucky you have Tucker. She's one of the best parents I've ever met. I worked with teen parents for years, but when it's your own baby, you second guess everything."

"She was young when she had Bart," he said. "And I look at him, and I'm amazed at what a phenomenal kid she raised. If I can do half the job she did with him..."

His sentence died when Jace skooted off Eli's lap and said, "Eye," then toddled in his direction and sat on his lap with a decided thump.

"He said your name."

Tyler looked down at Jace who started chanting, "Eye, Eye, Eye..."

Tyler laughed. "I think we have a future sailor on our hands."

TUCKER GLANCED OVER at Tyler, Eli and Jace. Whatever they were talking about, Tyler was happy.

Seeing him relaxed made something in her ease.

"Eli will bring him around," their friend Laura said. "She's impossible to resist. I remember."

"She is a force to be reckoned with," Tucker agreed. One of the best things she'd ever done was to go to Eli then-Cartwright at school and tell her about the pregnancy. Eli had come with her when she told her father, and she'd stayed with her throughout the pregnancy, offering advice, finding programs that could help. "Yeah, a force of nature."

Laura nodded her agreement. "So, how long have you been hung up on him?"

"Huh?" Tucker asked, surprised by the question.

"Tyler," Laura said. "How long have you been hung up on Tyler?"

Tucker scoffed. "I'm not hung up on him."

Laura laughed. "If you say so."

Laura obviously didn't believe her denial, so she said it more forcefully. "I'm not."

"You don't have to argue the point with me. If you say you're not, you're not. I know what it's like to come to terms with falling for someone. You have to figure things out for yourself. Remember, when you're ready, I'm here."

"Wow, you marry into the Keller family and next thing you know, you're as mushy as the rest of them. They make you go soft in the head."

"No, they make you go soft in the heart."

Tucker rolled her eyes, but Laura only laughed more. "Just don't forget, we're all here. I remember a woman showing up in a snowstorm, wearing only a hoodie, bringing me food after I'd had Jamie."

"You're exaggerating. There was snow, but not a storm." Tucker had simply shown up with Eli.

"You have your version of events, I have mine. All I know is you hardly knew me, and were there for me. I'm here for you if you need me."

Laura's new husband, Seth, came up behind her and wrapped his arms around her. They'd both lost spouses, but had found each other. Laura had once confided that loving Seth had helped her heal. She'd worried it was too soon to fall in love again, but Seth had convinced her that it was never too soon for love. Their happiness was overwhelming. And watching them made something in Tucker twist. She glanced at Tyler, who was still talking to Eli.

"What are we talking about?" Seth asked.

"Tyler."

The normally easygoing man, frowned. "I know I'm going to sound suspicious and very police-like—"

"You're allowed to sound coppish...it's in your DNA," Laura assured him.

"I heard through the grapevine that he has a record."

Tucker knew there was no way this was not going to get out, but she felt bad for Tyler, regardless. There was something about the situation that felt off to her, but she couldn't pinpoint what, and she certainly couldn't defend his actions. "Whatever he did is in the past. He's served his time, paid restitution and works for us. He's been a stellar employee, and he's been loving to Jace. I'm willing to accept him on those facts. I hope you can, too."

Seth nodded. "I know better than anyone that you can't let you past rule your present and taint your future. I'll give him the benefit, but if you ever need me…"

She smiled at the Erie police lieutenant. "I know how to reach you."

Seth nodded, then grinned and said, "Rumor has it the dogs and burgers will be done in a few minutes."

"We'd better help Eli bring out the salads and stuff."

As if she'd heard them, Eli got up and left Tyler with Jace. She waved at them and joined them.

"He's a nice guy," she said to Tucker.

"He is," was all she said in response.

Tucker glanced back at him, and Seth had walked over and was talking to him. She was about to go run interference, when Colm joined them. The gentle man said something that had both men laughing and Tucker relaxed. It was fine. She'd been right to bring Tyler with her.

THREE HOURS LATER, JACE had conked out in his bed at Tyler's and they both stood at the doorway, watching him sleep.

"We should think about redoing this room," Tucker whispered.

"What's wrong with the room?"

It was barren other than a small dresser and the crib. The walls, while clean, had once been white and had aged into a cream color. The hardwood floor was a bit nicked, but basically in good repair, though it could benefit from an area rug to soften the feel.

"Nothing's wrong with it, but Jace is going to be living with you, the room should look like a little boy's, not like some makeshift guestroom."

Tyler frowned and appeared to be studying the room more critically. Tucker rushed on with her ideas. "Maybe a coat of paint, an area rug, a toy box and..."

He nodded. "Make it a little boy's room."

"Yes. I'd help."

Tyler's frown deepened.

She resisted the urge to stamp her feet. She'd spent her life in the company of men, but they still could be the most aggravating people. "Stop. I thought that if I took you to the Kellers you'd get it."

"Get what?" he asked.

"That it's okay to rely on others. It doesn't unman you, or make you weak. You're not losing anything—you're gaining. That's what the Kellers are like. They celebrate everything, but more than that, they support each other without question. You talked to Seth, right?"

"Uh-huh."

Tucker continued. "He spent a few years apart from the family. He didn't cut them off, but he held them at a distance. I'm not sure exactly

116

what it was all about, but when he got together with Laura, whatever it was got fixed. I saw him before, and I've seen him since, and he's a completely different person. Standing on his own didn't make him stronger, it made him lonely. Relying on his family, that's what made him stronger."

"So what you're saying, in your own so subtle way, is I should let you help paint Jace's room?"

"Listen, Bart wouldn't be who is today if I hadn't had people to rely on. My dad, Eli, the guys at the shop. That's what Jace deserves. This is about more than a coat of paint in his room."

"I can do it on my own," he maintained.

Tucker recognized stubbornness when she saw it. She'd grown up with her father after all. He still managed to throw out getting a partner comments whenever he had a chance. She was pretty sure that bullheadishness was a gene that attached to the Y chromosome. Maybe it wasn't just bullheadishness. Maybe it was pride. Patiently, she acknowledged he was right. "You *can* do it on your own, but you don't *have to,* and I've decided that I'm going to take my own advice and I'm going to take you up on your offer."

"What offer?"

Pride wasn't related to gender. She certainly had some. Possibly it was time to set it aside as an example to him. "Well, actually, I was going to barter with you. I'll still help with Jace, while you look for a reliable sitter in Whedon, and you'll do some of the paperwork."

"I went to jail for embezzlement." His voice rose from their hushed tones, and he stalked down the hall and toward the kitchen muttering.

Tucker followed after him and caught the last part of his soliloquy. "What kind of person would let me anywhere near their books?"

Tucker caught his arm, and spun him around, then pointed at her t-shirt. It was baby blue and had a small yellow bird with googly eyes and said, *Crazy Car Chick*.

He scowled, but she could catch a hint of humor beneath his annoyance. "I'm going to have to start paying attention to your t-shirts."

She grinned, but didn't say anything as she waited for him to continue.

Finally, Tyler sighed. "Yes, Tucker, if the offer still stands, I'll take it."

She pushed her luck and asked, "With both the room and the babysitting?"

He nodded. "So, it's not only Bart who gets Angelina's life lessons, it's me?"

"It is. And can you tell me what your life lesson was today?"

"When someone offers to help, I should say yes?"

"Not all the time, but in this instance, yes. When people love your kid and want to help, you should say yes."

"He is mine now, isn't he? The thought still terrifies me."

"It should—at least if you were doing it alone, but in this case, you have help. You know what they say, it takes a village—or in this case a garage—to raise a child." She laughed at her own poor adaptation of the phrase. "It's okay to be single and a little hung up on your feelings, but when you have kids, they have to come first above everything else. So, what if we run to Home Depot and look at some paint tomorrow? We can start on the room. And maybe next week, you can take a look at my books and offer a few suggestions."

"You're pushy and crazy," Tyler said with no heat.

Tucker agreed. "I know. I think I have a t-shirt that says as much."

Tyler tried to look stern, but in the end, he laughed. "I'm sure you do."

TUCKER WAS ON TYLER'S doorstep at ten the next morning, Bart in tow. "The painting crew has arrived."

She'd made a run to the store and bought various shades of blue paint, and she'd also packed some of her tools of the trade, most notably her airbrush and a small, portable compressor.

Bart was handing a second load of things from the car.

"You gonna give us a hand?" she asked.

Tyler leaned over to pick up her compressor and stopped mid-way to stare at her chest.

She might have taken offense, but she knew he noticed her shirt. "I wore it for you." It showed a woman pushing a car up a hill and read, *Pushy Women Get the Job Done.* "It was a present from Lou."

Tyler chuckled and picked up the compressor. "How many t-shirts do you own?"

Bart came up behind his mother. "Way too many. I think both her dressers are filled with them. She has them organized by color and by age. The older ones are work shirts, the newer ones she considers dressy."

"This is an old one," she clarified, "'cause we're here to work."

"I'm here for a few hours, then I've got to go," Bart added apologetically.

"It's nice of you to do this. Both of you," he clarified.

"Don't fool yourself. Mom's not merely doing, she's in charge. She might let you think you're the boss. I mean, after all, it's your house, but she won't trust you with painting. We're her peons. That's it."

"Bart," she scolded. "You weren't supposed to tell him. I wanted to leave Tyler with the illusion of—"

"When you showed up with everything, I'd already figured out I was at your mercy. So what color are we..." His question trailed off as Bart started coughing. Well, actually, the coughing was an attempt to cover his laughter, but it didn't work very well.

120

"Color, Tyler?" Bart shook his head. "You really have never met Angelina Dorothy Tucker, have you."

"Wait a minute, Dorothy? Your middle name is Dorothy?"

"After Pop's mom. She was a very nice lady. Sweet and easygoing. They hoped some of her attributes would rub off on me."

"They didn't," Bart assured him. "Mom's sweet like a Sweet Tart. Big emphasis on the tart."

"You're calling your mother a tart?" she asked, her voice challenging.

"No one uses that word the way you're taking it, Mom," he assured her.

She stopped her mock squabble with Bart when she spied Jace sitting in the middle of the living room floor.

Jace stood and hurried across the floor, raised his hands at Tucker and babbled what was obviously baby orders to pick him up.

"Hey, big guy. What do you think about your bedroom getting a quick coat of paint?"

He reach out, grabbed one of her short curls and pulled.

"I take it that's a yes. Let's get to it, boys."

Later that afternoon, Jace was napping on a blanket on the floor in the living room as Tyler worked on painting a dresser on the porch. Bart had long since left, and Angelina was doing

121

something on the two-toned blue walls in Jace's room.

She'd asked if he minded a surprise, and he'd said no, so she'd banished him to the porch with a can of paint, the dresser and instructions.

He thought about her t-shirt and grinned. She was definitely pushy, but in the best kind of way.

He wouldn't have thought about painting the baby's room.

He glanced at Jace sleeping peacefully and despite the fact he continued to call him a baby, he wasn't. Jace was a toddler.

And Jace belonged to him now.

He understood the Matthews weren't capable of raising their grandson.

He understood it, but he was scared. Scared to his bones that their trust in him was severely misplaced.

What if—

"Hey, slacker, you done yet?" Tucker asked, pulling him from questions he couldn't answer.

He took another brush at the drawer for effect and nodded. "Done, ma'am."

"So am I. Come in and see what you think."

They tiptoed past the living room and the sleeping baby.

At Jace's bedroom door, Tucker asked, "Remember the other day when Jace was eye-eying all over the place?"

He nodded.

"Well, pair that with the fact we live on the doorstep of one of the great lakes, and..." She opened the door with flourish.

Tyler stepped forward and took it in. She'd had him help paint light blue on the upper part of the walls, and a darker blue on the lower half. On her own, she'd painted in waves, and clouds. The sun shone brightly near the window, and there was a huge sailboat taking up the biggest wall. He got closer and saw it was named Jace-Racer. And there were two people on the deck. "Me and Jace?"

She smiled.

"Angel, it's amazing."

"Thanks. My friend, Laura, has a big mural on her baby's wall. I thought it was cool. I wish I'd have done something like that for Bart. Since I didn't..." She shrugged.

"Laura. She's the one with...Jamie?" he asked, remembering the blond woman from the Keller house.

"Yeah, that's her. Her husband's the cop who grilled you. One of her students painted the mural as a gift, and I loved the idea, so..." She shrugged again.

He studied the walls and turned to her. He schooled his face into a serious expression. "I only have one complaint."

"Oh?"

"You should be on the boat with us. And Bart. You both did more of this than I did."

"We don't need to be on it, too. We're..."

"Unless it's too much work?" He knew Angelina would take that as a challenge.

She snorted. "No, it's not too much work."

He watched, as she got out a paint set and a small brush and drew in two more people on the deck with sure and easy strokes. Minutes later, there was a miniature Angelina and Bart next to him and Jace.

"Thanks," he said.

Underplaying her gift, she said, "It was nothing. It only took a moment."

"It wasn't nothing," he assured her. "And I'm not thanking you for only this, I'm thanking you for everything."

"You're fam—"

He cut her off. "You've made me feel a part of something I haven't felt in a very long time. I worked at the investment firm for years, and I wasn't ever anything more than employee. If I'd worked there another three decades, I'd still have never been more than a body to them. I walked into Tucker's Garage, and you all took me in when you had every reason to hold me at arm's length. I don't know how to tell you what that means."

Tucker looked uncomfortable. "You really want to thank me?" she finally said.

"Yes."

"Great. I accept your thanks, so stop thanking me."

"I don't think I can say it enough."

"If you want to thank me, then stop thanking me. You could, however, order a pizza. I'm starving and I'm officially inviting myself to dinner."

Before he could think of anything more to say, Jace squawked and Tucker hurried from the room, no doubt to check on the baby.

He stopped in the middle of the room and studied the sailboat. Jace, Tucker, Bart and him.

Almost as if they were a family.

Almost.

Perhaps once he could have had that dream, but now? He felt horrible that Jace would be raised by a man with a record, although it meant his father's name was unblemished, at least. Tyler could take comfort in that. But he wouldn't let anyone else share the burden of his name and conviction. He knew what it was like to be tied to a man whose name was tarnished.

Almost would have to do.

ON MONDAY AND TUESDAY, the whole shop took their turn with Jace. Angelina had the morning shift, then each of the guys sat with him while they rotated their lunch breaks. Watching North trying to teach Jace to do a Vulcan sign was about the funniest thing Tyler had ever seen.

Mr. Tucker went to sit at Angelina's house while Jace took a long afternoon nap. Angelina confided he had a soap opera he enjoyed.

Bart helped out after Jace woke up.

125

It was a hodge-podge way of caring for a kid, but Tyler loved knowing that Jace was close at hand and surrounded by people who loved him.

He didn't doubt that part.

If Tucker's garage had been quick to absorb him into their arms, they'd moved even faster with Jace.

On Wednesday, when he'd finished the BMW he'd been working on, Tyler headed over to Angelina's to collect Jace.

Tyler heard raised voices before he'd even reached the porch and his stomach roiled. He hesitated before knocking on the door.

"Come in," Angelina called. "Have a seat and give me a sec. Jace is sleeping."

She turned back to her son. Bart towered over her, and was obviously as upset as she was.

Tyler took a seat, but sat on the edge, poised to make a fast getaway with the baby if need be.

"You know you're supposed to call." Angelina's voice was filled with anger. He'd never heard her like that. She practically radiated with it.

Bart threw up his hands. "I forgot, so sue me."

"I don't need to sue you." Angelina took a step toward him and waggled her finger up at his face. "I have so many other options. I can ground you—you might be eighteen and all that, but you still live here, in my house. I can take away your car privileges. Or how about I take your phone? How will you communicate with your girlfriend

126

without a cellphone? You'd have to—" gasping, she held a hand to her mouth for dramatic effect "—use the landline."

"Mom, I said I was sorry. I mean, what do you want from me? I can write it in blood if you think that would help."

"You did say you were sorry, but you said it as if I were the worst mother in the world to insist you tell me where you are and what you're doing. How hard is it to call and say you'll be late?"

"I'm eighteen."

Tyler remembered his last fight with his father had been on the day he'd turned eighteen. He'd stayed at the Matthews' house most of his senior year of high school. He hadn't seen his father in months. His stomach churned harder at the memory. His father had hit him, and for the first, and only time, he'd hit him back before his father could continue the beating. He'd left then and had never looked back.

Until now.

Nervously, he tried to focus on mother and son.

"You are eighteen," Tucker agreed. "Which means you do know my cell number, and I'm sure, judging by the amount of time you talk to whoever this new girl is, you know how to use the keypad either to call or text me." She jabbed at an imaginary keypad for emphasis. "Just pick up the damn phone and tell me you'll be late. Let me know you're not dead in a ditch."

"Why on earth do you always go there if I'm a little late?" Bart asked, then muttered, "Drama queen."

"Drama queen?" Tucker sputtered, as if looking for something to say that would counter his accusation. "Have you read the statistics for teenaged drivers?"

"I'm not a freaking kid anymore."

Bart's voice was still loud, but the angry edge had faded, as if he was finally understanding what his mother was saying. As the tension between them ebbed, Tyler felt himself relax a bit.

"No, you're not. You're old enough to care about someone else's feelings. In a few months you'll be gone to college. You'll be independent. I get that. I remember what it's like to feel as if you're an adult for the first time. But a real adult would realize that being courteous isn't a sign of immaturity. Worrying about someone else's feelings shows exactly the opposite."

She turned and asked Tyler, "If you were going to be late picking up Jace, you'd let me know, right? You wouldn't leave me here worrying?"

"I don't think I want to get in the middle of this."

She turned back to Bart. "Ha. That's Ty's polite way of saying, he'd call. Because he's an adult. Because he wouldn't leave somebody hanging, especially someone who cares." Tucker reached out and gently touched Bart's forearm. "I worry because I care. I've spent eighteen years worrying, and it's going to be a tough habit to break. I won't make you report in at college, but when you're here, when you've said you'll be home at one time and then ignore phone calls and texts, and don't show up until two hours later—"

Any residual anger bled off, and Bart seemed truly apologetic. "I get it and I really am sorry, Mom."

Angelina seemed to relax as well. "Well, okay then."

"I'll call next time," Bart promised.

"I'd appreciate that." She stood on tiptoe and kissed his cheek.

It was so tender, so loving, Tyler felt a pang of longing. Would his mother have loved him that fiercely if she'd lived, or would she have been like his father?

"So, what's for dinner?" Bart asked.

"Taco lasagne."

Bart leaned over and kissed her cheek in return. "I guess there are worse things than having someone worry about you."

"I guess there are. And while you're feeling so mellow, I should probably warn you that if you don't call at least once a week while you're in college, I'll worry. If I don't hear from you, I'll drive down to Pittsburgh."

He laughed and started down the hall. "So, if I get homesick, I *shouldn't* call...got it."

"Smart ass," she called after him.

She turned back to Tyler. "Sorry about that. Jace is napping and..." The sentence faded off and she looked concerned. "What's wrong, Tyler?"

"You two were fighting and then you weren't. Just like that."

"Yeah, we were fighting. Bart went out and said he'd be home by two-thirty, but he didn't walk in until right before you did. I'd tried calling, but he'd had his phone on vibrate, and then left it in the car."

"But you were fighting, then you were talking about food." When his old man fought with him, well, it didn't end in a dinner discussion.

Angelina was staring at him as if he were slightly crazy. She nodded slowly. "Uh-huh. We fought. Bart apologized and will probably remember next time. At least for the next few times. There's a chance we'll have a similar fight again before the summer's over, and probably when he's home for his first holiday break. But eventually, it'll sink in. My future daughter-in-law will appreciate the efforts I made."

Tyler shook his head. He felt mystified. "I've never seen a fight like that."

"You're new at the garage. It would have happened sooner or later. Pop and I used to get into some major rows..." She paused. "You've never fought like that?"

"No. I'd get mad at Jason. He was like my brother, so okay, we occasionally annoyed each other, but we never fought. The one time we did, I ended up taking a swing at him."

She whistled. "He must have done something really boneheaded because I don't see you being prone to that kind of thing."

"You don't know me." She kept looking at him as if she did. But she didn't. And for the life of him, he didn't understand her. She was pissed her old man hired an ex-con, then suddenly was acting as if it had been her idea all along. Hell, she was trusting him to help with their accounts, even though she knew what he'd gone to jail for. What was with her?

"I don't really know you, but I'd like to," Tucker said slowly. "So tell me. Tell me about you and fights."

"I don't do it with people, not even normal arguments, because I don't know how to do it without someone getting hit."

"Your parents?" she asked softly.

Tyler shook his head. "No. My mom...she died when I was ten...my father was a drunk. A mean drunk." He let his explanation rest there. It was apparent that she understood what he was saying without him going into graphic detail. He remembered odd incidents. The day he'd used the last of the milk on some cereal, and the old man—hung over as usual—went to get some for his coffee. That time the authorities had questioned his father, who said his son's broken arm was the result of a fall.

As the social worker stood next to the bed, asking about the accident and if he'd really fallen, his father had stood on the other side of the bed waiting for Tyler to agree with his version. Tyler had been maybe fifteen. He'd wanted to tell the social worker that his father was lying. Sure he'd fallen—fallen down the stairs—but only because his father had pushed him. In the end, he'd nodded his head in agreement; telling the truth wasn't a luxury he could afford.

Tucker reached across the table and put her hand on his. "I'm sorry. But fights don't have to end up with someone getting hit. And I maintain that Jason must have done something truly stupid if you reacted violently. That is not the Tyler Martinez I know."

"But that Tyler Martinez is the one I live in fear of. I've spent every day of my adult life trying not to be my father's son. Not to live down to the name he'd given me. It was easier when it was me, on my own, but now there's Jace—and there's no way getting round him. What if I'm like my old man, Angel? What if Jace comes in late, and rather than have a fight with him like you did with Bart, what if I smack him across the face, then toss him down the stairs the way my father did to me?"

"You won't." There was so much certainty in her voice.

"I might. I've read that people parent the way they were parented. And my father's SOP involved an open hand if you were lucky, and a fist if you weren't. I know I wouldn't be able to live with myself if I ever raised a hand to Jace."

He raked his fingers through his hair. "I didn't want this," he said with a burst of anger. "I had my life planned and it didn't involve raising someone else's child—ever. I don't want to screw up Jace, but I know if Jason were here, I'd be apt to deck him for a second time. None of this is happening how I expected it to."

Angelina pulled her hand away. "My first instinct is to whap you upside the head and say, *idiot,* but somehow I think that would be counterproductive, so instead, just sit there and listen."

She got up, paced and didn't say a thing.

"Angel," he started.

She shushed him and continued walking around the table for another few seconds, then stopped to face him. "The first thing I need to say is, taking in Jace wasn't what you planned, but it's what you've done, so now you've got to deal with it. I'm going to tell you to shut up, suck it up and figure it out because those are the exact words my Pops used when I had Bart. Neither of us planned being responsible for a kid, but life is what it is, so now you've got to stop whining."

"Whining?" He wasn't sure if he was insulted or amused by her choice of words.

She shrugged. "Whatever you want to call it. It's done. Jace is yours, for better or worse. And that leads me to the second thing—you love Jace. It's written all over your face every time you pick him up. At first, you probably loved him 'cause you had to, because he's your best friend's kid and you were his godfather. But now, it's there. As clear as the nose on your face. You love him like I love Bart. Completely and all encompassing. I'd throw myself on a grenade for my kid. You'd do the same for Jace. That's something. Something big."

"But what if *I'm* the grenade that explodes all over him?"

"Shh," she said again. "You love him too much and you're too smart for that. But me saying that probably won't make you worry less, so let me add this—if you ever lay a finger on that baby, now, or when he's Bart's age, I'll step in and even take you on, Martinez." She stood, hands on hips, looking fierce. "I might be small, but I'm scrappy."

Something in him melted. She was such a petite woman. Tiny even. And yet, he believed her. She'd take him on and she'd win. She'd never let him hurt Jace.

Never.

His relief spread at the thought.

Angelina Tucker would never let him turn into his father.

He reached out, took her by the hand and drew her into his arms. "Thank you," he said before he kissed her.

He kissed her with all the hunger he'd felt when he'd first asked her out. He'd hardly known her then, all he'd known was that he was attracted to her. Now, he wanted to know more.

He wanted to go on kissing her and more.

Much more.

The sound of a door slamming somewhere in the house reminded him they weren't alone and reluctantly, he pulled back.

"Well," was all she said.

"Well," he echoed because he didn't know what to say either.

She saved him from finding something else to say by asking, "So, you'll stay for supper?"

He nodded. "I'll set the table."

And just like that, they bustled around her kitchen as if nothing had happened. Tyler tried to ignore the fact he never should have let it happen. She deserved her shot at freedom. She deserved a better man than him. He couldn't let it happen again.

But something had happened.

Something big.

CHAPTER SIX

"IT'S OFFICIAL," TUCKER declared to her friends Eli and Laura on Friday night.

One of the many nice things about being adopted by the Keller family was the occasional girls' Friday night out. When Eli and Laura's other sisters-in-law were in town, they sometimes joined them, but most of the time it was the three of them.

Eli and Laura were both teachers and both had young children. They said getting together on a Friday night every once and a while was sometimes the only thing that saved them after a crazy week. Tucker generally sympathized with their small-kid-woes, but Bart was, for all intents and purposes, an adult now and she'd forgotten what it was like coping with little kids...until now.

"What's official?" Eli asked.

"I've lost three pounds in the last two weeks chasing after Jace. I officially remember what's it's like to take care of a toddler. All those other Friday nights out with the two of you, I've commiserated and I've sympathized, but I was

136

faking it. Blatantly faking it. I'd forgotten how intense toddlers can be."

"You're still babysitting?" Eli asked.

Tucker had expected her friends to be amused by her statement. Instead, both looked concerned.

"Yeah. We did the same kind of baby-balancing act when Bart was young, and it's all come back to us—to the whole shop. Of course, Joe and North weren't around back then, but they've caught on fine. As a matter of fact, North offered to buy Jace his Halloween costume."

"It's only barely July." Laura's expression finally indicated the amusement Tucker had been hoping for.

Feeling encouraged, Tucker continued, "North's got to special order it."

Laura smiled, as she asked the proper question. "What is North thinking of making Jace?"

"Baby Spock." Tucker had shared North's love of all things Star Trek with the women before, so they all laughed. "I told Tyler it was his decision. If he gives North free rein on this, next thing you know, Jace will be in his teens and North will be teaching him to speak Klingon."

Eli smiled at the statement, but her expression quickly turned serious as she asked, "Is Tyler still looking for a sitter?"

Tucker nodded. "But it's summer. Whedon's one daycare center is overflowing with younger kids who are on summer vacation. The same holds true for private sitters around town. And it's not practical for Tyler to drive all the way into Erie each day, then back to work." She didn't add that the truth was, she hated the thought of Jace going to a babysitter. She'd fallen head over heels for the baby.

She'd had Bart while she was still in her teens under less than optimal circumstances. She'd doubted many things about her parenting abilities, but she'd never doubted for one instant how much she loved being a mother.

She knew she wasn't Jace's mom, but every time he reached for her or called her Uck, she melted. She didn't mind not being married, or in a serious relationship, but she was wishing she'd had more children. She was beginning to wonder about adopting a baby. The Kellers had adopted their whole clan, and look how well that had turned out.

Eli's voice was sharp and pulled Tucker from her baby-adopting daydream. "So, Tyler expects you to limp along like this until fall?"

Tucker eyed her friend. Eli had always been the most easygoing of women, until now. "What on earth is up with you?"

Eli looked primed for a fight. "Tyler's using you. I don't like it."

Laura was a new friend, and it was obvious she wasn't comfortable with the turn this conversation was taking. She sat quietly in the booth and practiced looking invisible.

Tucker focused on Eli as if she'd grown horns. "Tyler's not using me. You know me better than that. He never asked, I offered. And truth be told, it wasn't so much an offer as an order."

"You've told us over and over again how busy you've been at the shop. More and more people want you to paint their cars and bikes."

"So?" Tucker challenged.

"So," Eli said slowly, "now your dad's retired and you're in charge of everything, you're adding a lot to your plate even without the babysitting."

"Tyler's helping with the accounting duties. He's finding ways to streamline the paperwork process." Tucker felt it made for an even exchange. She'd much rather cuddle a squirmy toddler than balance a ledger.

"Yeah, because that makes a ton of sense," Eli scoffed. "Give an embezzler a shot with your books."

Laura broke her invisibility by murmuring, "Seth will go crazy if he finds out."

"So, he doesn't have to find out. It's no one's business how I run the garage." Tucker was ticked off. It wasn't up to her friends to judge how she handled her business. "I've never seen you two like this."

"We care about you," Eli said.

Tucker's annoyance over their attitude warred with the warmth over their concern that prompted it.

"I guess you're going to have to trust me and trust my judgement. Tyler's not what you think."

"So, convince us," Laura said.

"I—" Eli began, but Laura sent a be-quiet-and-listen look in her direction and she snapped her lips shut.

"Tyler's..." Tucker hesitated, not sure how to describe him in a way that would change Eli and Laura's opinion of him.

Her silence seemed to be all the invitation Eli needed to unsnap her lips. "I remember a couple years ago when he was asking you out. I was angsting over the age difference between me and Zac, and you were telling me about a guy who kept wanting a date. You felt you were too different and wouldn't give him the time of day. What's changed?"

Tucker started to say Tyler'd changed, but she wasn't sure that was the truth. Oh, the clothes he wore and the car he drove had changed, but the essence of who Tyler Martinez was hadn't. "Maybe I've simply had an opportunity to figure out who he is, who he was, beneath the fancy clothes and car. He's kind and caring. You should see him with Jace. Assisting me with the shop's books wasn't some nefarious plan on his part. He even told me I'm a fool to let an embezzler anywhere near them."

"But—" Eli started.

Tucker cut her friend off. "And as for me watching Jace, like I said, I offered. I listen to you two when we go out, and I miss Bart being that age. I'm not really interested in relationships, not to mention there's a whole other host of things I don't excel at. But I'm great in a garage, with a paintbrush in my hand. And I'm equally good with kids. I'm enjoying myself. Sure, it's hard work juggling Jace's care, but it's worth it. He calls me Uck."

"Uck?" Some of the tension eased noticeably in her friends and they both grinned.

"I wasn't sure he was talking about me the first time he said it, but you can't miss it now."

"I don't think I'd be that impressed with being called Uck," Laura said.

"Hey, there could have been other variations of Tucker that would've been worse. A lot worse."

Laura and Eli both laughed, and the rest of tension that Tucker had felt evaporated. "Okay, what else is on our evening's agenda?"

They finished their dinner then went to a movie. Tucker lobbied for a new action/adventure, but found herself sandwiched between Laura and Eli as they both grew teary-eyed at the romance they saw.

Normally Tucker could laugh off a good romance as unrealistic, but tonight's movie left her feeling strange. She and Tyler were spending so much time together because of work and Jace. She'd told her friends how much she enjoyed Jace, and that was true. She loved watching him toddle around the house, and seeing him change each day. Whether it was saying her improvised name, or adding a new block to his tower. She couldn't get enough of him. She'd been working a lot of evenings to make up for her days with Jace, but she didn't mind that. Bart was busy with work, his new, as yet unnamed, girlfriend and his friends. He was gone most evenings and the house got quiet.

Too quiet.

Going back over to the shop gave her something to do. It filled up her evenings. She'd flip her iPod onto shuffle and enjoy singing out loud with her favorite tunes as she designed and painted one project or another.

She liked the new rhythm to her life.

No, it wasn't Tyler taking advantage.

She wanted to help with Jace. She'd fallen for the toddler.

As for Tyler? Images of the movie's hot love scene flashed through her mind as she drove home that night, only it wasn't the actor and the actress she envisioned. It was her and Tyler doing those things to and with each other. Things that left her with a physical longing she hadn't felt toward a man in a long time. She shouldn't be thinking like that.

She liked Tyler. Liked him a lot. He'd opened up a little to her about his father. She sensed that other than Jason, Tyler had never really shared that with anyone. But there was still a lot she didn't know about him.

But she was certain of one thing, there was more to his embezzlement story. She wasn't sure what, but the idea of skimming money from his employer and clients didn't fit the man she was beginning to know.

The man she really wanted to know more of.

LATE MONDAY MORNING, Tucker admitted a long-since-cooled-off cup of coffee in her hand wasn't enough to stop her from glaring at the stack of receipts and bank statements in front of her. Heck, even the fact it was the Fourth of July and she was going to the fireworks later didn't help ease her dislike of the paperwork.

Honestly, she didn't understand people who chose careers that involved doing spreadsheets and math all day, every day...on purpose.

"Payrolls, warranties, inspection forms," she muttered under her breath, like a mantra. No, more like a curse. There was no end to it. "Ordering invoices, preparing estimates, finalizing bills...figures, forms and fun, oh, my..." she continued, with a cadence from the Wizard of Oz's lions, tigers and bears, oh my.

"Ah, what're you up to, Angel?"

She spotted her father in her doorway watching her and smiling. She growled a greeting, which only made him laugh.

"Ah, paperwork. It does put you in a lovely mood, daughter."

"I can handle it, Pops."

"So, have you given any more thought to a partner? Someone else who had a stake in the business who wouldn't mind the paperwork."

"Like I said, I can handle it, Pops. I can handle everything."

He came into her office with far less nervousness than the guys would have shown. They all tended to disappear quickly when they caught her doing paperwork.

Her father didn't show any such fear as he sat down opposite her. "Angel, I know you can handle everything. You've spent your entire adult life handling everything that was thrown at you. Not only handling, but triumphing. You are an amazing woman and I'm so very proud to be your father. But that being said, you are not meant for an office. You're an artist. You need to play to your strengths."

Her father frequently called her an artist, but that felt presumptuous to her. "I'm a mechanic who does a bit of painting."

"You're more than that, and we both know it. We have people lined up to have you customize their cars and motorcycles. You've put Tucker's Garage on the map. Don't think I don't realize that it was you and your work that took a small local garage and turned it into a place that people drive miles out of their way to come to. We specialize in all kinds of vehicles now, as well as your customized paint jobs. That's where you belong—in the paint room, or in your office, but designing. You don't belong behind a desk doing," he reached across and picked up the paper in front of her, "inspection forms."

"Pops, I—"

He cut her off. "I know what this is, and it's my fault."

"What what is, and how is it your fault?"

"After you got pregnant with Bart I lectured you about responsibility, about standing on your own two feet. I still stand by that, and you've more than proven that you can do it all, but just like with Bart, you can ask for help, Angel. More than that, you can accept help. You can share this workload." He ran his fingers through his thinning, grey hair. "Hell, you can share your life with someone else. I worry I made you think relying on someone else somehow lets me down."

Was it her imagination or was it thinner? His face showed signs of aging—lines she didn't recall him having a year ago. That couldn't do his heart and his health any good. "Pops, you're wrong. I know how to rely on people. As a matter of fact, I've never done anything on my own. Like you said, I've had you, the guys. Every single one of them. Look how they're all pitching in with Jace."

If her father has been frowning before, he was practically scowling now. "About that."

Tucker's worries took a backseat as she sensed a lecture coming on. She felt her hackles rise, even before he said another word. She tried to tamp it down for her father's sake.

Her father ignored it. "Are you sure you haven't taken on too much by caring for a baby on top of everything else you do...?."

"Pops, I'm enjoying Jace. And you know it's not only me. You've come over every afternoon to watch your soap and listen for him while he naps."

"I don't watch soaps," he protested, then added, "and that's different. I'm retired. I can play surrogate grandpa if I want. You're too busy. I thought babysitting might remind you there's more than the garage. I thought it was short term. I wanted you to find a life, not take on more work."

"Pops, you can't have it both ways. You can't tell me to let other people in, then tell me I don't have time for it. And Pops," she added gently, "this isn't up for debate. In the fall, it will be a lot easier to find an appropriate sitter. We've got some feelers out. Eli is talking to Mrs. Keller and she knows absolutely everyone in Whedon. This isn't permanent. But I'm not going to let Tyler dump Jace with someone because it's timely or convenient."

"You have a say in something like that? About who Tyler leaves the baby with?" her father asked. "What is going on with you and Tyler?"

"We're friends." He eyed her in his very discerning fatherly way. "Friends, Pops. But I like Jace as much as you do. I heard you talking to him the other day about going fishing, then I caught you in the shed. I'm betting that bag I saw you carry out had Bart's old kiddie fishing pole, didn't it?"

"Maybe, but be that as it may, I'm going to tell you now, Angel, that when I hired Tyler, it wasn't with the idea of him dating my daughter in mind. He's a great guy, and I believe in second chances..."

"It's okay to have him work here, but not to date me?"

Rather than look chagrined at the hypocrisy, her father nodded. "That's absolutely right. I don't want you and him dating."

"You don't think I'm old enough to decide who I want to date?" Before he could answer that question, she asked, "And how did we move from me bringing in a partner, to me spending time babysitting Jace as a favor to a friend, to my fictional dating of Tyler Martinez? He asked me out a ton in the past and I've always said no, so why do you think that would change now? And to be clear, he hasn't asked me out since he started working here."

"I've seen how you look at him, and how he looks at you. There's something there. There was something there a couple years ago. When I asked you why you said no, you said he was a charmer who wears business suits, as if that were an answer. Well, daughter, he's not wearing business suits now." He nodded his head for emphasis.

Tucker knew that her father was here because he loved her, because he worried about her. But that was the last thing he should be doing. He didn't need the stress. "Pops, I love you, and I love that you care, but I've long since stopped needing your dating advice. And to be clear, I'm not dating Tyler."

"Not officially dating him, but you two are together a lot. And I've only commented on your dating one other time—that was with Bart's father. We know how that turned out."

That was a direct zing. "Ouch," she said.

He looked apologetic, as if he knew he wasn't fighting fair. "I want better for you than a guy with a record."

"Pops, I'm not looking for a man. Bart leaves for school this fall, and for the first time in my entire adult life, I'll be on my own. Responsible for myself. Unencumbered. I'm not interested in something serious or permanent with a man— with any man," she reiterated. "As you've pointed out, I have enough on my plate with the business. But if there comes a day that I don't have time for a friend..." She left the sentence hanging because she didn't know how to finish it. She knew she'd always find time for a friend.

And Tyler was a friend. "So, that's that, right?" she asked. "I don't want to have this fight with you or with anyone else again."

Friday night her friends, today her father. What on earth was going on?

"I love you, Angel. I've spent my whole life worrying about you, and that's not going to change. You'll see when Bart goes to college. You'll still worry."

"I know you're right on both counts, Pops. And I love you, too."

"So, are you going to put aside your papers there and go into town for the fireworks?" She'd forgotten it was a holiday until she got into work this morning and found the garage deserted. Then Tyler had called.

She decided not to mention that to her father. "I had plans to go into Erie for the fireworks, and you're welcome to come along, too, if you like."

"I wasn't fishing for an invitation," he told her. "As a matter a fact, I'm taking Marilyn out for the evening. They're having some a polka band down at St. Stan's."

"Pops has a girlfriend," she singsonged. "That explains your worry over my dating habits. You were hoping I wouldn't notice you're dating someone."

"Angelina," he warned.

She laughed. "I'm bustin' 'em for you, Pops. I think it's great. Isn't she the Bentley Continental GT?"

He nodded. "Yeah."

Tucker let out a long, low whistle. "You picked a classy lady. She's always been very nice to me."

"It's some polka music, dinner, then the fireworks."

"Do we need to have a discussion like I'd have with Bart, about dating and what could happen and being safe?"

Her father looked as uncomfortable as she'd felt earlier. "You're funny, Angel. Very, very funny."

She was giggling as he walked away.

She heard the murmur of voices outside her office door and wondered who else had come into the shop on a holiday.

She thought about getting up and checking, but the inspection form her father had tossed onto her desk taunted her. She sighed and picked it up.

Paperwork was the bane of her existence.

TYLER STARED AT ANGELINA'S father.

"You heard?" George Tucker asked.

Tyler nodded. He'd heard Angelina's proclamation that they were friends. She hadn't dated him when he'd had money, why would she date him now that he was simply a mechanic? Not that he'd ask her to date him. He wouldn't drag her into his mess.

"Yes, I heard, sir. And Angelina's right, we're friends. Only friends. She's been wonderful with Jace. So have you and the other guys. The daycare center in town is willing to take him. I can see about arranging it." His stomach turned at the thought of putting Jace into such a big center. Ideally, he wanted to find someone grandmotherly. Someone whose only focus would be Jace. The baby had lost so much. He

150

deserved to be someone's singular focus while Tyler was busy fixing cars.

"No." George shook his head. "That's not what I want, and I know it's not what Angel and the other guys want. We can continue this for a few more weeks until you find the right place for him. We all love him now, and don't want anything less than the best." He paused and added, "I feel the same way about my daughter. She deserves nothing but the best."

"I understand, sir." And he did. Angelina deserved the best, and anyone with half a brain would know that was someone other than Tyler Martinez. "We're friends."

"Fine then." George clapped Tyler on the shoulder. "I'm very glad you're working here. All the guys have nothing but good things to say about you. You're an asset to the business."

"Thank you, sir."

"I believe in second chances," George continued, "but I can't believe in them where Angel's concerned. I hope you understand that."

"I have Jace now, and I guarantee that I get it. Even before he was in my care, I wanted nothing but the best for him."

"Okay. I assume Angel was waiting for you?'

In the interest of being honest, he told Angelina's father, "I'm meeting Joe and North in Erie for dinner and the fireworks. Joe's bringing his wife, and the idea of another in-depth Star Trek vs. Star Wars discussion with North was almost more than I could stand. I invited

151

Angelina to come along and run interference. It wasn't a date, though. It was all the guys and Jace..."

"It's fine, Tyler. If you can pry her away from her desk and get her out of here, I'd appreciate it. She's a very stubborn woman."

Tyler snorted. "I've noticed."

Angelina threw open the door and said, "I heard the words *stubborn* and *woman* and assume the two of you were discussing me?"

"Tyler says he's taking you into Erie with him and the boys."

"I know, I said yes," she said to Tyler, "but really, I have a ton of work—"

He interrupted. "I could use a hand with Jace. I haven't really tried an outing with him, and rumor has it you're an expert."

"Where is he now?" she asked.

"Bart was leaving when I came in and Jace wanted nothing to do with anything that didn't include him, so they're out in the front looking for bugs. He ate one the other day."

"Bart?" she asked with a grin.

Tyler chuckled. "No, Jace. I called poison control, but the lady there assured me he probably wasn't going to suffer any serious side-effects from chewing on a spider."

"Oh, gross," Angelina groaned. "Bart ate a slug once. Pops said think about it as a protein source."

"Bugs aside," Tyler said, "you're still coming?"

She eyed her father, who smiled at her, then she turned back to Tyler. "Fireworks sound wonderful."

"Thanks. You're saving me from North's enthusiastic science fiction talk."

"Oh, nothing can truly save you from that. But hey, maybe we can scope out the celebration and find a woman for him. Someone who likes guys who have big sci fi tattoos?"

"You think that such a woman exists?" Tyler asked.

"We'll ask Joe and Carol to keep an eye out. Maybe with all of us looking..."

Angelina's father said, "Have fun you two, but not too much fun."

Tyler wasn't sure if George's warning was for him, or for Angelina, but he knew her dad was right, having too much fun with Angelina wouldn't do.

DESPITE THE ODD TENSION between her father and Tyler at the start of the outing, Tucker was having fun.

They all gathered at The Cornerstone for dinner before heading down to Erie's bayfront for fireworks. North stayed behind with a girl he'd met...a girl he'd met with Tucker's help. She had watched North and their waitress, Jen, flirting with each other all evening, half-envious of them. It had been a long time since she'd been that young and felt that first rush of attraction. And she wasn't sure she'd ever flirted.

Then she glanced across the table. It was strange to be with Joe outside the garage. They didn't do this kind of thing often enough. She hadn't seen Joe's wife, Carol, in a long time. But watching them together gave her the oddest feeling, especially when she saw them holding hands. Knowing they'd been married for years and still held hands...

She'd sighed when she noticed, then felt appalled. She wasn't a sigh-over-mushy-displays sort of person.

She blamed Laura and Eli's chick flick on Friday.

After dinner, Joe and Carol drove to the fireworks and they eventually lost them in all the traffic. Tucker was relieved. North's infatuation, Joe's mushiness with Carol... Tucker was just as glad to escape the chick-flick-worthy public display of affection.

Tyler and Tucker parked on Front Street, packed everything in Jace's stroller and walked to the bluffs that overlooked Erie's bay. Once an industrial hub, the bayfront was now a tourist destination. A big outdoor amphitheater, a convention center and a huge tower at the foot of the dock anchored the ever-growing and changing landscape of the bay.

They found a small grassy spot and spread Tucker's red and black checked blanket. Eating out with everyone had tired Jace to the point he practically collapsed as soon as they'd settled.

It was a warm July night, filled with the hustle and murmurs of the crowd that was gathering. Tyler wasn't saying much. As a matter of fact, he hadn't said much all night, so they sat in silence waiting for the fireworks. The city was launching them from a barge in the middle of the bay. They had the perfect view of the water. From high on the bluff, Tucker relaxed as the humid summer evening turned darker, the city below them lit up and boat lights bobbed on the water.

She forgot about her father's lecture and her friends' concerns. She forgot about paperwork and the new van she was supposed to paint a mural on. She forgot it all as she listened to the other people on the bluff murmur their conversations, and the occasional pop of someone's home fireworks.

"Penny for your thoughts?" Tyler finally said.

"My thoughts?" She wasn't sure she'd been actively thinking about much of anything. "My mind has been sort of quiet, but if I had to share a thought, I'd say I think it's beautiful out here. Whedon is so close to Erie and the lake, but I get so busy I don't take the time to come enjoy it very often. I'm really glad I came tonight. Thanks for asking. It's been a perfect evening."

"I can't believe you picked up a woman for North."

How could she have missed the way North had stared at their waitress? "Jen was cute, and asking when she got off work and if she was going to see the fireworks wasn't much of a set up on my part. North was the one that suggested they meet up."

"You started it." Tyler couldn't hide his amusement.

"Maybe I should reconsider my career choice and become a matchmaker?"

"I think there would be a lot of car and motorcycle buffs who'd hate it if you did." He paused. "By the way, I love the T-shirt. It's not exactly car or motorcycle oriented like most of your collection."

She looked down at her T-shirt that read *The Big Bang*. It had fireworks exploding from a central point. "I thought it was appropriate for the day. And I have other styles of T-shirts, although most are related to cars and motorcycles. Customers pick them up for me. I swear, I think Lou has my size posted somewhere around the garage as a hint. But I have other interests. Don't tell North, but I'm a closet science geek who happens to really love science fiction, too. It's a closely guarded secret."

"Why don't you tell him? When he noticed your shirt and started talking about The Big Bang Theory show, you teased him."

"You bet I did. You've seen the way Lou, Joe and Pops pick on North. You think I want to risk my secret getting out? I'd never admit I love that show, and that I frequently understand their geeky references *before* they explain the joke to the non-geek masses." It was one of the few shows she DVR'd.

Tyler laughed. "So, basically what you're admitting is that you throw North under the bus?"

"Nope, I throw him under the UFO." Tucker knew it was a stupid joke, but Tyler laughed even harder and she joined in. She was relieved that they seemed back to normal. "Ha, I look like a closet sci fi geek, and you look like you're a preppy, just like when we first met. You're all khaki and polo shirty. Sunglasses propped just so on your perfect hair."

SITTING HERE ON THE bluff, overlooking Lake Erie with a beautiful woman and a sleeping baby, Tyler had forgotten George Tucker's warning until Angelina's reminder of who he had been, which led to him thinking about who he was now

Tyler knew Angelina was kidding, but he couldn't help frowning at the reminder of when they'd first met. Back then, he'd thought he had everything he wanted. The good job. The suits. Driving an Audi S5.

Before.

"Oh, Tyler, I'm sorry. I didn't mean to remind you..." Angelina left the sentence hanging there between them.

157

"Finish the thought, Angel. You didn't mean to remind me that I threw that life away? That I lost everything that I was back then? That I'm a convicted criminal?" Even if he could go back in time and do things differently, he wouldn't. He couldn't. Although knowing that he did what he did for a good and worthy reason didn't make his fall from grace any easier to handle.

He'd always thought he'd build a different, better life for himself than his father had. And yet, here he was—practically following in his father's footsteps. Working in a garage, a kid to take care of, and a rap sheet.

He was a chip off the old block.

"There's something about your...uh, situation that's been nagging at me," Tucker said hesitantly, which was not her standard operating procedure. She was a throw caution to the wind and speak her mind sort of woman, so her reticence stood out.

"My situation?" he asked.

"There's something you're not telling me." Then more to herself than to him she murmured, "There's something not right about it."

He chose his words very carefully. "Angel, I went to court and stood before the judge and didn't fight the charges. I took a deal."

"See, that's just it. You *didn't fight the charges* and *took a deal.* Did you tell the judge you did it? Did you actually say it?"

He hadn't. It was a point of pride. One of the few remnants he allowed himself.

Tyler didn't lie. He might be a chip off the old block in a lot of respects, but not like that. After each of his benders, his father would swear that was the last time he was done drinking. And every time his father hit him, or beat him, he'd swear that he'd never touch him again.

Lies.

Tyler had to hold on to at least one truth about himself if he could help it.

So he couldn't lie to Angelina as she looked at him so trustingly. He had never admitted to the crime, he simply hadn't contested the charges. Maybe it was splitting hairs, a fine line, but it was a line he drew and could walk. It was a line that allowed him to live with himself. That was the part of the plea deal he'd insisted on. He wouldn't plead guilty.

She took his silence as a sign she was right. "Told you. You'd never do something like that."

"You're wrong, Angel. If it was Jace," *or you,* he added silently, "I'd do anything it took. Anything. I'd beg, borrow or steal if I had to." In his heart he knew it was true. He'd break his last promise to himself and lie if that's what it took to protect one of them.

"I think I understand that. I'd do anything for Bart." She paused and added, "You're a good man, Tyler Martinez. I don't need you to tell me what happened. I want you to know, I believe in you. You're a good man."

It was too much. Too damn much. Angelina sat across from the baby wearing her sciencey, holiday t-shirt and jeans, and looking at him as if he'd hung the moon.

She believed in him. With no proof. Heck, with nothing at all. She simply believed in him. Before the formal charges were even made, friends and colleagues had abandoned him. They'd believed the worst, but not Angelina.

He'd wanted her since the first time he'd seen her. She'd crawled out from under his car with a smudge of oil on her cheek, her hair tucked into a baseball cap, with fly-away curls escaping every which way, and she'd grinned at him.

He generally dated other professionals—women who were more at home in cocktail dresses than jeans. But one look at Angelina Tucker, and he'd pursued her with an instant lust that wouldn't give him respite.

When it became apparent she wasn't interested, he'd swept that desire under the rug, but it was back now, stronger than ever because now he knew her and she was amazing. Walking into the garage before, he'd felt the same sense of accomplishment he always did when someone else serviced his cars. He loved to wait at the shop and visit with George Tucker, knowing that he didn't have to touch a wrench or a lugnut. But George hadn't been there that day, only Angelina.

He didn't understand it then, but he did now.

Now, it had gone beyond that initial immediate attraction. He cared about her, more every day. Watching her tonight at dinner, laughing with her friends, blowing on french fries before handing them to Jace, talking with such excitement about the fireworks, like a little girl. And his desire grew.

Like a dash of cold water, he thought of George Tucker telling him that Angelina deserved more than an ex-con.

If only George knew the truth. It wasn't simply his conviction that made Angelina Tucker out of his league, it was everything else.

He should scoop up Jace and get away from her. He started to move toward the sleeping baby, when Angelina intercepted him and kissed him. She instigated it, and controlled it, taking that simple kiss and turning it into something profound.

There was hunger in her kiss, but there was tenderness, too.

And that tenderness was his undoing.

All his fine ideals and plans to walk away faded beneath the weight of that tenderness. There, over the sleeping baby, he kissed Angelina back trying to say in that one gesture what he would never say in words.

A loud boom over the bay pulled Tyler back to reality, and regretfully, he broke off the kiss. "I think we should watch the fireworks."

Another boom broke loose. Tyler felt the sound reverberate in the pit of his stomach. Or maybe it was the enormity of what he'd done.

What he was doing.

He was falling head over heels for Angelina Tucker, and he couldn't let that happen. He was about to say as much when she interrupted his thoughts, "You're not saying it, Ty."

"Saying what?" He waited, sure she was going to want to talk about their kiss and try to make it mean more than he could ever allow it to mean.

"*Ooh. Ahh.* That's the only proper response to fireworks. You take turns with them."

A large orange firework snowballed in the sky. "*Ooh,*" Tucker said.

A group of small, white fireworks zipped to and fro after it. "*Ahh.*"

He forgot about warning her off.

Tyler Martinez forgot about all the reasons he needed to stay away from Angelina Tucker. He simply sat back and watched her enjoying the fireworks, *oohing* and *ahhing* along with her, although he knew she was *oohing* over the fireworks and he was *ahhing* about what he couldn't have.

He'd told her about his father, and she'd assured him she would never let him turn into his father. She'd protect Jace.

But it wasn't his father's physical abuse that hurt the most, it was the memory of how he'd treated Tyler's mother before she died.

Sometimes, secretly, Tyler thought his mother died because she finally gave up. Gave up hoping, gave up dreaming, gave up believing in anything.

He knew what that was like. He could have given up back then as well, but he'd had a friend in Jason when he was growing up, and now, after losing Jason, he had Angelina.

He had her as a friend.

He liked her too much to let it be anything more than that. He continued to watch her as they *oohed* and *ahhed.*

When he'd first asked her out, he'd been casual about it, figuring that's what would appeal to her.

He knew her better now, and knew despite her penchant for funny t-shirts, there was nothing casual about Angelina Tucker.

And more importantly, there was nothing casual about his feelings for her.

Which is why that last kiss was *the* last kiss.

She deserved more than he would ever be able to give her. She deserved a man with a sterling reputation. A man without a past. She deserved love, laughter and a lifetime of happiness.

None of that was in the cards for him. He was, despite all his attempts, and hers, his father's son, and Angelina Tucker deserved more than that.

And he cared enough about her to see to it that she got everything she deserved.

CHAPTER SEVEN

TUCKER FELT AS IF SHE were playing some strange tug-of-war with herself...and with Tyler.

One moment they were kissing with fireworks crashing overhead and the next moment he was treating her as if that kiss that had blown her socks off had never happened. As if she were a bosom buddy as they dealt with Jace's needs.

Two weeks of it.

Tyler would pick up Jace from her each day after work and practically sprint to his car. He'd hand off Jace the next morning minutes before he needed to start work, leaving no time for any uncomfortable conversations.

She looked down at the T-shirt she'd found on her workbench this afternoon. A long haired man in a black robe on a motorcycle with the words *I Ride, Therefore I Am* emblazoned on it. Underneath the main caption was a tiny caption that read, *What Descartes Would Have Said if He Had a Harley.*

Tyler had left it with a simple Post-it. "Saw this and thought of you. It's a small thank you for all your help with Jace."

The T-shirt was perfect—the Post-it was generic.

Tucker sighed as she fingered the soft cotton shirt. Tyler treated her as if she had the plague, but knew her well enough to know how much she'd love a T-shirt that combined motorcycles with philosophy.

The only meaningful conversations they'd had since the Fourth were about Jace and the business. Tyler was building a new set of online templates that were supposed to speed up the process.

Her father had never changed his methods since she was small. Tyler was bringing Tucker's Garage's books into the twenty-first century. He waxed poetic about the Excel program he'd set up.

She looked at the T-shirt in her hand. He'd seen it and thought of her?

She wondered if he thought of her as often as she thought of him. She was making herself crazy behaving like some lovesick teen. Not that she was a teen or anyone had said anything about love.

Now, lust, that was an entirely different matter. No one had said anything about that either, but she knew she had an acute case.

She stared at the delivery van that sat in the center of her paint room.

It was done. A stylized mural for a local bakery. Cakes, pies and cookies that looked almost real enough to eat. She'd painted a lot of things, but never food and she was pretty pleased with her results. She had a motorcycle that was due next week, but it was only a howling wolf on the tank and some pinstriping. Nothing taxing. She didn't need to start it tonight.

She'd caught up on her paperwork. Well, not caught up exactly, but she wasn't so far behind that she needed to keep at it into the wee hours. She could go home and veg in front of the television and watch shows that she enjoyed since Bart wouldn't be in until late.

Owning the remote should be a treat, but instead she sighed. Bart coming in late was pretty standard this summer. He worked as a lifeguard at the Sunrise Foundation's daycamp a few days a week, helped with Jace on his days off, and every evening he disappeared with friends. They drove into Erie and went to the peninsula, or the mall.

She got that. In fact, she encouraged that. She remembered that feeling of exhilaration when she graduated from high school. She would have loved running around with her friends that summer, but she'd had Bart. She'd grown up quick and while she didn't regret anything to do with her son, she wanted him to have it easier, so she didn't mind his having a great senior summer. She simply missed him.

Okay, so no Bart to distract her from thoughts of Tyler this evening.

She couldn't even go out with Pops. He was out with Marilyn. Again.

Too bad Jace was with Tyler. She could have loaded him into the stroller and taken a walk.

Maybe she should get a dog.

Her thoughts skittered from one option to another, but no matter what kind of distraction she came up with for her evening, what she really wanted to do was see Tyler and Jace.

No. Tyler and Jace were out. She could call Eli. She discarded that idea as well. Eli had a family now. Zac, Ebi and Johnny.

With no clear plans, Tucker started shutting up the shop. She turned out the lights in her paint room, then headed into the main garage. A light was burning at Tyler's work station.

She walked over to turn it out, too, and spotted a piece of garbage tucked behind a toolbox at the back of the work table. She'd expect to see debris on Lou's bench, or even North's or Joe's, but Tyler was meticulous, about himself, and his tools. The balled up paper seemed incongruous. She picked it up to throw it in the trash, and realized it was an envelope.

A certified envelope.

Tucker laid it on the work bench and flattened it out.

It was an unopened, certified letter addressed to Tyler.

Maybe it was something important and he'd forgotten it.

The polite thing would be to take it over to him, right? And her father had always taught her to be polite.

After she'd dropped off Tyler's letter, she could see if he'd mind her borrowing Jace for a walk. She used to love walking Bart through Whedon on dusky summer evenings. More often than not, he was sound asleep before she got back to the house.

Tyler would probably love having someone else put Jace to sleep.

Even though she knew that the envelope was a weak excuse, she felt better than she had all day. Showing up on Tyler's porch because her house was too quiet was lame. Showing up because she wanted to kiss him again, lamer yet. But dropping off a letter that could very well have some kind of significance, well, that was simply a kind gesture and not lame in the least.

She made the drive to his house in record time.

As always, she was struck again by the incongruence of the house he lived in and the house she'd always imagined him living in. Although it was a bit rundown, it was as neat as everything else about him. Everything but the letter that she was taking to him.

Now that she was here, showing up on his doorstep uninvited, she felt awkward. Then she glanced at the letter in her hand and knocked on the door.

It took a little longer than she'd anticipated for him to open it. "Angelina?"

"Tucker," she reminded him, though she didn't know why she bothered. He might remember for a minute, but he'd forget and revert to referring to her as Angelina soon enough. It would bother her if it were someone else. But for some reason, she didn't mind that Tyler called her by her given name, and only corrected him out of habit.

"I found this at the garage." She held the wrinkled envelope out to him. "It looked important, so I brought it over."

Tyler turned and walked into the house and she assumed that was an invitation and followed. "Where's Jace?"

"Sleeping. Bart and your dad had him out fishing this afternoon and he didn't get his nap. He was so tired he fell asleep in his spaghetti. I took a picture before I cleaned him up and tucked him in. I figured you'd like it."

"I would. I have a picture of Bart when he was about that age. He fell asleep while eating a chocolate ice cream cone." A sense of wistfulness struck her anew. Her son was no longer a toddler who fell asleep in his food. He was an adult who was building his own life—one that didn't revolve around her.

"I was going to ask to take Jace for a walk, but guess not." She realized she was still holding the envelope and held it out to him again.

He didn't take it.

"Is it important?" she asked.

"No," was his monosyllabic response.

And his denial told her the opposite. "Do you want to talk about it?"

"No." And as if suddenly recalling his manners, he added a very formal, "Thank you."

She didn't know what to do with the envelope, so she simply set it on the small table by the doorway.

"Tyler, what's with you? One minute we're buddy-buddy, then we're kissing on the bluff, and then you're treating me like..." She shrugged, not sure how to define the wall he'd put between them. "Did I do something?"

"Your father made it clear he doesn't want us dating."

"Here's a news flash—my father doesn't make my decisions."

"Maybe he should, because you should want more than I'd be able to give you. You deserve the whole nine yards. Hell, you deserve..."

Tyler let the sentence fade as he stared at Tucker as she closed the distance between them.

So close. She was so close to him, but she still felt the distance he'd worked so hard to maintain the last two weeks. She wasn't sure why it bothered her so much, but it did. She was tired of being held at arm's length when all she wanted to do was get closer.

She was tired of her father and Tyler telling her what she should want. What was best for her.

Tucker wasn't accustomed to taking orders from anyone. She'd forgotten that for a moment, but she remembered now. She reached up, locked her fingers behind Tyler's neck and gently pulled him down so that his lips were an inch away from hers. She heard him sigh and sensed whatever war he'd been fighting with himself was over. He met her lips with his own.

The other kisses they'd shared, even the hot one on the Fourth, suddenly seemed chaste when compared with this one. This kiss was something so much more and it went on and on, which was fine with Tucker.

She could have stood forever, locked in this embrace. But obviously Tyler couldn't. He pulled back and then took a couple steps to separate them. "Walk away, Angel. This is all I can offer you."

"What? A kiss that about blew my mind. I don't think something like that is settling."

"It is, because for you it should be more than sex. And I can't give you more than that. Friendship, yes. That's already yours. But nothing more. I'm an ex-con with a kid. You've been a single mother your entire adult life and when Bart leaves for school in a few weeks, you're finally going to have a chance to be on your own. To explore what you want out of life. To do what you want when you want. You deserve that."

"Do you really want to give me what I deserve?" she asked. When he nodded, she said, "Then let's take this into your bedroom, please."

"Angel, I..."

At first, she thought he was going to say no, but then he took her hand and led her up the stairs.

AN HOUR AND A HALF LATER, Tyler wondered about the woman sleeping on the other side of the bed.

What the hell had he done?

Angelina deserved so much more than he could give her—he'd said as much repeatedly to himself, and to her—and yet, here they were. He watched her and wished more than anything that things were different. That he wasn't turning into everything he hated about his father.

An ex-con, for all intents and purposes, a single parent, a mechanic and a man who saw nothing wrong with using women.

His father had been a user. Tyler lost track of the number of women his father brought home in a drunken haze. Nameless women who his father discarded with no thought or remorse.

Tyler had never done that.

Any woman he dated understood he wasn't interested in a long-term relationship.

That's what he'd intended back when he'd asked Angelina out. Two people having a good time. And if she'd said yes back then, maybe that would have been all they had. Maybe not. But now, he knew that she wasn't like that. Despite what she'd said downstairs, she wasn't the type of woman who could separate sex and love.

Not that he was conceited enough to think she loved him. But he knew that she cared for him, and this was part of their lovemaking.

What the hell had he done?

Jace squawked in the next room. Thankful for an excuse to get out of bed, Tyler rolled to his side, but Angelina stopped him. "Let me, please? I think that's one of the things I miss the most. Getting a baby in the night."

"Sure," he said and kept his gaze on her as she got out of bed and reached for her panties and her ever-present T-shirt, then hurried next door.

He laid back in the bed and listened to her murmur to the baby. He couldn't make out what she was saying, but Jace was quiet.

About ten minutes later, Tyler got up, slipped on his jeans without fastening them and padded next door. Jace's bedroom door was ajar and he peeked in.

In the soft glow of the small lamp, Tyler could make out Angelina sitting in the rocking chair, the once-again sleeping baby in her arms. His legs hung over the arm of the chair, and his one arm draped over the other end, but Angelina didn't seem to notice. She rocked and stroked Jace's white blond curls, singing so softly Tyler couldn't make out the song.

She looked up and smiled at him and Tyler realized how big a mistake he'd made by making love to Angelina.

He'd worried about her feelings. He'd worried that she couldn't separate and compartmentalize having sex and keep it from spilling into deeper emotions. And now he realized it wasn't Angelina with the problem. It was him.

He couldn't separate his feelings from making love with her.

It was love.

Pure and simple.

Well, not simple. Not simple at all. He stood there lost in watching her cuddle Jace and though he couldn't regret losing everything when he went to jail because he'd had to do it, at this moment he wished it had never happened. He wished he'd grown up with the Matthews family, and not with his drunken abusive father. He wished that he was standing here a man without all the emotional baggage, able to give Angelina Tucker everything she was due.

"Ty?" she whispered.

"I was checking on the two of you. I'll be downstairs when you put him back down."

He padded barefoot down the stairs and into the kitchen. If he was a drinking man, he'd pour himself a glass of something about now. But he didn't. Not ever. His father's example was too much of a deterrent. He settled for making some coffee. Normally he wouldn't think of his favorite brew this late at night, but he knew he wouldn't be sleeping anyway.

He listened to the coffee perk and stared out the window. The fireflies that had been so prevalent this summer blinked on and off merrily in the yard under the huge silver maple that only allowed the merest of dappled moonlight to shine through.

He loved the peace of this farmhouse. It was the first place he'd felt at home since that brief time he'd spent at the Matthews' at the end of high school.

He could hear himself think here.

What he was thinking tonight was that he was a fool to act on his desire for Angelina.

He heard her come into the room, but still stared at the backyard.

"Penny for your thoughts," she finally said, repeating his line from the Fourth of July.

"They're not even worth half that much," he assured her without turning around. Maybe if he didn't look at her he could end this here and now—end it without her knowing that it was the last thing he wanted to do.

"Maybe they're worth a lot more than that to me. Talk to me, Tyler." She stepped between him and the window, forcing him to look at her. "Talk to me."

"What do you want me to say, Angel? I was honest when I told you this couldn't be more than sex."

"And I was honest when I said I was okay with that."

How did you fight a crazy woman who didn't even begin to realize her own worth? "It shouldn't be okay with you, Angel."

"Yeah, you keep saying that. But since that's all you'll allow, I'll find some way to settle. I mean, here I was secretly pining for a white gown and wedding ring. You *know* how I'm very into that kind of froo-froo stuff, but somehow I'll survive. I'll cancel my subscription to Bride's Magazine and—"

He turned away from her again and slammed his open hand on the counter. "Dammit, Angel, this isn't funny."

"Oh, and I know this routine. You're going to tell me how tough you are. How afraid you are that next time I piss you off like magic you'll turn into your father and smack me." She closed the gap between them and stood next to him without actually touching him. "Well, here I am, Tyler. Not crying, sobbing and telling you I can't live if you won't make an honest woman of me. Not backing up and not backing down. I'm probably upsetting you left and right. And to be sure I am, let me ask again, what was with the registered letter?"

He remembered his mother pulling in on herself when his father came home drunk. Afraid

176

of a wrong step that would set him off. Angelina didn't have that sort of internal censor. She seemed to revel in pushing him. "What is wrong with you? You're like half my size. If I did hit you, I'd flatten you."

"That's a huge *if.* To be honest, I don't really think it's an *if* at all. It's a possibility I don't believe in. Not for one second. You've spent your life worrying you're going turn into your father, but it won't happen. Not ever. I know with absolute certainty that I could push you to the edge of reason, and you'd still never hurt me. Ever." She stood there, fearless and ferocious in her belief in him.

"How can you know that when I don't?" he asked softly.

"Because you see yourself through a filter...your father stands between you and your true reflection. I simply see you—only you—and you would never hurt me."

"Angel, you're nuts."

"Yeah, I've heard that before." She reached out and wrapped her arms around him and simply held him with the same kind of tenderness she'd held Jace with. "I'm not asking you for anything more than you can give."

"What if I say I can't give you the answers you want?"

He felt her shrug as she still embraced him. "Then I'll wait until you can."

"And if I never can?"

"Like I said, I'm pretty sure I see you more clearly than you see yourself. I'll wait." She snuggled even closer. "But what, oh what, will we do while I'm standing here waiting?" She glanced up at the clock on the microwave. "It's only nine. Bart's curfew isn't until eleven thirty, so I have some time to hang around. That is if you can think of something to do to keep me occupied."

He planted a kiss on her forehead before he thought about it. "You're insane, you know that?"

"And you are one smooth talking man whose sugary words could win any woman's heart." She stopped and laughed. "Not that you want to win my heart. But maybe I could convince you to try winning my body again before I have to go home?"

The coffee pot sputtered to the end of its cycle, but Tyler could have cared less about that cup he was craving moments ago.

All he could think about was this foolish, trusting woman who wouldn't see sense. A woman who trusted a man convicted of embezzlement with her business's books. A woman who believed in him despite all the evidence to the contrary.

Standing there in her classic T-shirt, with sleep-tousled curls, she smiled at him as if she knew she'd already won.

Hell, maybe she did know him better than he thought.

He leaned down, picked her up and started toward the stairway.

"Put me down, you're going to break something."

He snorted. "Like I can't handle a pint-sized woman like you."

"Pint-sized, my ass."

"I can handle that, too."

She laughed. "If you break something, don't come whining to me."

Tyler laughed as well, but he realized he was at risk of breaking something. Not anything physical. But when he let Angelina go—and he would have to let her go eventually—he'd be breaking his own heart.

But she should have all those things she'd scoffed at. She should have a ring and a white dress. More than that, she should have a man who would love her and treasure her, and never hurt her. She might think she knew him, but he knew himself better—he wasn't that guy.

As he took her to his bed for a second time, he vowed it was the last time. Simply, he was saying goodbye.

TWO WEEKS LATER, TYLER was still vowing every time he was with Angelina it would be the last. And if it had been any other woman, he would have made it stick. But Angelina didn't take no very well.

Actually, she didn't take it at all.

He'd say something like, "Tonight it would probably be best if Jace and I bached it."

And an hour later, she'd be at his doorstep hammering a cheery tune. They took Jace for long evening walks and then gave him his bath before story time and tucking him in.

Angelina had bought out half the Whedon bookstore. She explained that reading to kids early and often helped them do better at school. Tyler started letting Jace pick a story before they left for the garage each day. He didn't manage to insert the same level of enthusiasm into his storytelling as Angelina did, but Jace didn't seem to mind.

One morning, Angelina had pulled out an old wooden toy chest that had been Bart's. It was painted with every kind of vehicle imaginable. Cars, trucks, motorcycles. Big equipment like bulldozers and back hoes. She filled it with some of Bart's old toys, and new ones. Every time Tyler turned around, Angelina was buying a new book or new toy for Jace.

Jace called, "Eye-Eye," in that excited sort of way that pulled Tyler immediately from his work. He hurried across the room and kneeled down by Jace who pointed at the toy box.

Tyler knew this game. "Dump truck."

Jace pointed again. "Police car." Point. "Bus." Point...

It was a game that would last as long as Tyler was willing to play. He glanced back at the invoices he'd hoped to finish and then simply gave in. He'd stay late if he had to in order to finish them. Angelina would say babies first, paperwork after. "Harley."

Angelina hated sitting at the desk, while he found comfort in it. Give him a column of numbers and he could add it up with certainty. One and one were always two.

It was the rest of life that was iffy.

"Eye-Eye," Jace demanded, pointing.

"Wagon..."

TUCKER STOOD IN THE doorway watching Tyler with Jace. He'd been naming vehicles for at least five minutes nonstop. Jace toddled around the toy box, pointing and trusting that Tyler would answer.

Trusting Tyler. Jace trusted him, and so did Tucker. She'd thought her father would have a cow when he discovered she'd let Tyler help desk-jock-eying, but he seemed to trust Tyler as much as she did where the books were concerned.

It was only with her that her father drew a line.

A line she ignored.

Tyler himself drew the same line, but she simply kept crossing it. She'd had boyfriends before, but never let things get too serious. Tyler and his don't get-too-close warnings should be her perfect guy. But every time he warned her off, she got pissed.

He looked up. "Hey."

"Hey."

He glanced at Jace. "Have to stay a little late tonight. I want to finish those invoices."

"I'm not worried about it, Ty."

"I am. If you pay me for eight hours, you get eight hours."

"So, why don't I take Jace back to the house with me and we'll make dinner while you give me that last fifteen minutes of work you owe me."

She leaned down to pick up Jace, and Tyler gave her a tug that pulled her into his lap. He kissed her.

She welcomed the kiss and only broke apart when Jace wormed in between them.

She scooped up the baby and mock-scolded Tyler, "You know, you better be careful about kissing the boss. There are laws about that."

"I think you'd have more to worry about than me."

She laughed and she kissed his forehead with an easy comfort he found disconcerting.

"Yeah, I'm worried," she assured him. "Very, very worried."

"Eye. Uck," Jace said, squirming around on her lap, as if determined to get their attention.

"We're going to squish Tyler," Tucker warned.

"The day I can't handle a pipsqueak girl and baby—" Tyler started.

Bart was standing in the doorway laughing as he interrupted. "I can't believe she let you call her pipsqueak and live."

Tucker scrambled to her feet, Jace in her arms. She felt awkward being caught by her son. "We were just..."

Bart saved her from trying to explain. "It's okay, Mom. I stopped in to ask if I could have the car. Cessy called. There's a whole group of us who want to head into Erie for a concert on the Bayfront and I have the biggest car."

Tucker cleared her throat.

"Uh, *you* have the biggest car. So, can I borrow it?"

"You know the rules."

"I can't take more kids than I have seatbelts, and no horsing around while I'm driving. No phoning or texting. You know, I'm not a new driver."

"More accidents happen to drivers under twenty-one than any other age group, so you're new enough."

He sighed. "You'll still be giving me advice when I'm thirty, right?"

"Being a kid might end when you turn twenty-one, but being a parent goes on and on and on..."

Bart shook his head, a smile marring his seriousness. "You like lecturing, but because I'm a good son, maybe I can help spare you a lecture by giving the heads-up that Pops is on his way over."

Tucker took a step away from Tyler, putting more distance between them. "Thanks. Home by midnight, okay?"

"No problem, Mom." He turned and left with a quick wave behind him.

Hoping to avoid an uncomfortable confrontation with her father, Tucker scooped up Jace and started toward the door. "I'd better head up to the house. I'll try to intercept Pops."

"Your father doesn't scare me, Angel."

She drew her shoulders back. "He doesn't scare me either. I thought you'd work faster without the distraction."

With Jace on her hip, she made it as far as the hall before Tyler called, "Angelina?"

She turned around. "Yes?"

"Your father doesn't scare me, but he's right. We should end whatever this is between us. The Matthews are coming into town and they'll be helping with Jace. Maybe that will give you some time to think about what's happening here."

"We're friends...with benefits. I'd rather keep you as a friend, as for the benefits, well, if you've stopped wanting me?"

Tyler wanted to lie, but he couldn't, so shook his head. "Not even close to it."

"Well, then..." She grinned and wiggled an eyebrow suggestively.

"But you should stop wanting me and start looking for someone else."

"I've looked at men for my entire adult life...and I never have a problem letting go when

184

the time comes. I simply don't think that time has arrived for us. Not yet."

"Soon, Angel. The time should arrive sooner rather than later."

She didn't bother answering him, and made it into the work area before she spotted her father. "Hey, Pops."

"Angel. What're you and Jace up to?"

"Dinner at my place."

Her father glanced around, as if expecting to see someone. "Where's Tyler?"

"Finishing up some paperwork in my office."

She waited for him to say something about Tyler handling the books. But he didn't, so she waited for him to warn her off—again. He didn't do that either. Instead he came over and took the baby from her arms. "Hey, champ. Want to go fishing again tomorrow?"

Jace babbled a happy response.

"Do you mind?" her dad asked.

"It's not for me to mind. Tyler has to..." She realized it had been a trap.

"Well, then, I'll go check with him and let you and Jace get back to making dinner." He plopped the baby back into her arms and strode for her office.

"No one ever said he wasn't sharp," she muttered to Jace as she walked toward the house.

TYLER LOOKED UP as Angelina's father walked in.

"So, you're still helping out with the paperwork?"

"Angelina isn't a fan of doing it, and given all she's done for me..." He shrugged because there was no way to repay all she'd done for him.

George Tucker checked over his shoulder, then turned around and said, "She seemed mighty at home with that baby on her hip."

"Yes. She's great with Jace. I've learned a lot from her about coping with a toddler."

George nodded. "She was a good mom. Is a good mom. Even when she was so young, she was good at it. I always hoped she'd find the *right* guy and have a passel more kids."

Tyler didn't miss the emphasis on right. "She deserves nothing less."

George Tucker stood quietly, studying him, nodding. "I came in to ask if you minded me taking Jace fishing again tomorrow."

Angelina's father was an enigma. He gave Tyler a job when no one else would, helped him out with Jace, but recently gave him looks that said he didn't trust him. No, that wasn't fair. George trusted him with everything but Angelina, and Tyler understood that.

"Fishing tomorrow is fine. His grandparents are arriving on Wednesday."

"The visit will do them both good." The older man turned to leave the room.

"Mr. Tucker," Tyler called.

"Yes?"

"About trusting me with the books. I swear I'd never—"

"I know that, son."

"How?" Tyler simply didn't understand the entire family. Mr. Tucker might not welcome the thought of Tyler with his daughter, but other than that, he'd treated Tyler well and made him feel like part of the family.

Angelina's father gave Tyler a look that made him think of Angelina. "How what?" he asked.

"How do you know that I'd never embezzle from you?"

"Listen, second chances are important in life and I'm also a good judge of character. I don't know why you did what you did, but I believe, at heart, you're an honest man. And I believe you care about my daughter too much to ever steal from her."

Tyler felt humbled by George's faith in him. "Thank you, sir, I—"

Before he could sort out how he felt, George Tucker added, "And I come in every now and again and check your work."

Rather than feel insulted, Tyler grinned. "Good for you. Angelina should do the same."

"My Angel, she likes to think she's all tough. But between you and me, she follows her heart every time. But that's okay because she's got a lot of people watching out for her. Me, Bart and any of the boys in the shop would take a bullet for her. We've all got our eyes on you."

"Fair enough. I'm glad to know someone's looking out for her, because frankly, she's too trusting."

"Or, she's simply an even better judge of character than her father. I'm still trying to decide. Until I do, like I said, we'll all keep our eyes on you." George Tucker started for the door, then added, "And Tyler, it's not the business that has me worried the most."

"It should be."

"It's not. If we lost everything and the garage folded, we'd be fine. But if my daughter gets hurt...you won't be." That warning delivered, George Tucker left the room.

Tyler felt relieved that his work had been double-checked. But he felt anything but relieved about Angelina and her heart because no matter that he couldn't seem to give her up, he knew he was the wrong man for her.

She hadn't realized it yet. Hopefully, soon, she would.

When she did, he'd let her go with her heart intact.

He knew his wouldn't be.

CHAPTER EIGHT

"THE MATTHEWS WANT to see you," Tyler said without preamble Friday morning.

Jace's grandparents had arrived on Wednesday as planned and Tucker hadn't seen Jace since.

It had been a crappy couple of days.

She should be whizzing through her work without having to care for Jace; instead, she was putzing along, missing him. It felt odd to come into the shop first thing in the morning and stare at her sketch pad, trying to come up with some cool new design for Pisano Wholefoods Restaurant's delivery van. They'd asked for something they could reproduce as part of a new logo. She loved the idea of taking her work beyond vehicles and really wanted to nail this one. But she couldn't come up with a single idea.

Nada.

Zilch.

She wadded up the piece of paper she'd basically been doodling on and uttered the most articulate response she could come up with to Tyler's proclamation. "Huh?"

"Mr. and Mrs. Matthews would like to see you. They remember you from Jason's funeral. I've told them about you—about how much you've done for Jace," he clarified.

"Of course you told them about me *and Jace.*" Oh, she could hear that conversation— Tyler raving about his benevolent employer who put herself out for Jace's benefit with no mention of what was going on between him and her.

She pushed her sketch pad away with a bit more force than was necessary.

"What's wrong with you?" he asked, looking mystified.

"Men," she assured him. "I've spent my entire adult life working with men, but I still can't fathom how you all survive because the entire male species is clueless."

"Gender, not species," he corrected, grinning as if he thought he could jolly her out of her funk. He couldn't. She simply stared at him. Well, it was more than a stare and more of a glare. "Seriously, Angelina, have I done something?"

"It's more what you didn't do than something you did do." He still looked clueless so she spelled it out. "You told the Matthews all about me, and about how I've helped out with Jace, but I'm betting you didn't mention you were sleeping with me or that we had more than an employer-employee relationship."

"Of course I didn't. I mean, it's not like you've announced our..." He stumbled, as if searching for the appropriate word to describe what they had between them.

"Relationship, Tyler. It can be a relationship even if it's only friends with benefits. A relationship doesn't have to mean love and long-term commitments."

"What is wrong with you?" he repeated.

"Nothing. Not a darned thing."

He glanced down at her T-shirt. It was black, which matched her mood, and had a picture of a tire tread mark from one shoulder to the opposite hip with a motorcycle with teeth rather than a headlight and read, *Tread Lightly, I Bite.*

"Prophetic, or did you go change into it?" he asked, nodding at her chest.

"You're not funny, Martinez."

"So talk to me about what's wrong," Tyler said. "This mood isn't simply about what I did or didn't share with the Matthews. Tell me, Angel."

"Oh, I should talk to you? Fine. Let's trade stories. You tell me what was in that letter and I'll reveal why I'm in a less than pleasant mood." That shut him up, as she knew it would. She wasn't sure why that stupid, crumpled up letter weighed on her, but it did. She told him she'd be patient and wait for him to be ready to tell her, but she lied. She wasn't feeling patient about anything in regards to Tyler Martinez.

His silence stretched an uncomfortably long time. She finally said, "I guess we both have our secrets."

"So, about the Matthews?" he asked, obviously giving up on the idea of trading secrets.

"Given my current mood, do you think inviting me over to meet the parents is a good idea?"

"They're not my parents." His response was quick. Too quick.

And because she was in a mood, she didn't let the subject drop. She pushed. "They're as close as you've got."

"They're Jason's parents."

"And they love you as if you were a son, too. You met the Kellers. They taught me that blood doesn't make a family—love does. And I don't even have to spend another minute with Jace's grandparents to know they love you."

"How can you know that?" he asked.

It was official—Tyler Martinez was the dumbest male in the history of men. And that was saying something. "Ty, it's clear they love you because they've left Jace with you, haven't they?"

"They didn't have a choice."

"You're wrong, but then you're wrong about an awful lot of things." She sighed. "So when do they want to meet?"

"After work? We can cook out at my place."

"All right. Do you need me to bring anything?"

"Simply yourself. I'm asking the guys, and Bart and your father, too. The Matthews appreciate how much you all have done and they'd like to tell you in person."

"I don't mind meeting with them, and I'll even accept their appreciation gracefully, but know they're not the reason any of us is helping with Jace. You are."

"Yeah, I'm family, I know." Rather than sound pleased at the notion, he sounded as testy as she felt.

"Yeah, you are, and the Matthews are family, too. If I know you, you're freaked out about that as well."

He leaned forward so he was eye-to-eye with her. "Maybe you don't know me as well as you think."

"Oh, yeah? Does the idea of the Matthews thinking of you as a son freak you out?"

He stood back up and didn't answer.

"Ha. I knew I was right. And they've probably asked you to call them something less formal than Mr. and Mrs. Matthews. At the very least, by their first names, but I bet even if you've tried it, you've always reverted to Mr. and Mrs. Matthews. It's a way of maintaining distance. Emotional distance," she added, in case he didn't get her drift.

"Okay, Freud. Thanks for the analytical help, but maybe we could put away your couch this evening and simply enjoy ourselves?"

He started to walk away, and because talking to him hadn't made her feel less dark and dangerous—if anything it had only made her mood worse— Tucker called out, "Before I put away my therapist's couch, maybe you should ask yourself why, when you've done your best to maintain some distance with the Matthews all these years, you can't seem to manage it with me. I mean, you've talked about keeping things casual between us, but still insist on calling me Angelina, or Angel, rather than Tucker. That doesn't seem like maintaining distance at all—no matter what you say."

His spine was stiff, but he didn't turn around. He kept on walking out the door, which he slammed shut.

Good. She hoped she upset him.

She'd been in a mood since the Matthews came to town and he hadn't needed her for Jace.

No, if she were honest, she'd been in a mood since their last fight when she pushed and prodded him, hoping to prove to him he wasn't his father.

He didn't believe her.

She sat in her office, staring at the sketch book. Rather than thinking about her job, she started thinking about dinner. A picnic, that was casual. As for the Matthews—she didn't have a clue what to wear that was dressy enough, without being too dressy. She knew this particular T-shirt wasn't it.

She picked up her cell phone and texted Eli. *SOS. Need help picking out outfit for a picnic @ Tyler's aft wrk. Meeting parents.*

Half an hour later, probably during a break between classes, Eli texted back. *Don't sweat. Will be there soon.*

Feeling better, Tucker bent down to her sketch book and got to work.

Her mood was brighter. After all, she didn't have to cook tonight, she'd be seeing Jace, who she'd missed desperately, and Tyler was having her meet his surrogate parents.

All things considered, that wasn't too bad.

TUCKER TUGGED THE HEM of her sundress and glared at her sandals.

Asking Eli for help had been a mistake. Eli asking Laura for help helping Tucker only compounded the mistake. Laura had swung by the Millcreek Mall before heading out to Whedon with a new outfit for Tucker.

Then the two of them had done vile things. Torturous things. Things that they insisted had to be done in order to wear sandals.

Tucker had seen the nail-polish and files, and had thought they'd planned on simply painting her nails. It wasn't her favorite thing in the world, but she'd done it before.

But no. They'd done a pedicure. They'd clipped, filed and buffed, then painted her toenails.

She wiggled her toes as she got out of the car and cursed herself for asking for help.

She should have simply come in her T-shirt, jeans and workboots. She had the perfect T-shirt even. Lace is fine, but black T-shirts help hide the grease stains.

Yeah, she should have worn that one. But once she'd made the call and her friends had gone to all that trouble, she had no choice but wear the stupid dress.

No, not dress. Eli assured her that a dress would have been too fancy. A sundress was a step up from jeans and was very appropriate for a picnic.

What the hell had she been thinking asking her friends for help? Not that she needed to ask. She knew. She'd been thinking she wanted the Matthews to like her, and she'd worried that they wouldn't be comfortable with their grandson spending so much time with a work-boot wearing, glorified mechanic with a paintbrush.

Lou spotted her first and was wise enough not to say anything. He simply smiled in such a way that she knew he'd noticed she'd spruced up. He nudged Joe, who also smiled. Being married had given Joe an inner-censor on what to say and more specifically, when to say nothing at all.

Then North turned around.

North did not not have an inner censor. And he was far enough away that Lou and Joe couldn't serve as an outer censor for him as he whistled, long and low. "Wow, Boss, you clean up good. Why if I didn't work for you, I'd date you."

She slugged him in the arm. "You might ask me for a date, but I have taste...I'd say no. And there's the little age difference thing."

"Hey, I don't mind that you're old."

She slugged him again.

He rubbed his arm. "Old, but man, you don't hit like a girl, or like you're old."

She glared at him and he backed away, still rubbing his arm.

"Dork," she muttered as she moved closer to the house.

Jace spotted her then. He didn't care that she was wearing a sundress and sandals. He cried, "Uck," as he squirmed out of Mrs. Matthews's arms and ran to her in his toddley way.

"Hey, champ, I missed you," Tucker said as she scooped him up and hugged him.

He babbled a mile a minute, and she agreed with whatever it was he was saying and walked over toward Mrs. Matthews.

"Mrs. Matthews." She extended her free hand. She'd been introduced to the woman at Jason's funeral, but doubted his mother had registered her amidst the other mourners. "I'm Tucker."

"Tucker?"

She sighed. "There's a chance Tyler said my name was Angelina."

"Yes." Mrs. Matthews nodded. "He called you Angel a few times, too."

Tucker sighed. "I'd prefer Tucker, if you don't mind."

"I'll call you Tucker if you'll call me Marge." She dropped her voice and added, "My mother always insisted on calling me Margaret, but she was the only one. Well, my father would as well, but only when I was in trouble."

Tucker laughed. "I'm sure that wasn't that often."

Mrs. Matthews—Marge—gave her a wicked grin. "Oh, you'd be surprised. I was known to kick up my heels in the day, but since this last surgery, I'm not kicking much of anything." She nodded at the cane that was propped next to her. "I'm barely up and walking after the first surgery, and they're planning the second for two months from now."

"I'm sorry." Tucker couldn't imagine how hard it would be to have your mobility drawn up short like that.

"I'll be fine—seeking sympathy wasn't my intent. But I find it frustrating not to be able to do the things I used to do. Things I didn't even think twice about. And I wanted to say thank you. I've already told everyone else from the shop, as well as your father and son."

Tucker scanned the yard for them, but didn't see them.

"They're in the house with Bill and Tyler. You know, I'm not sure a mere thank you is enough for you."

"It's definitely enough, ma'am."

"Is it Angelina?" she asked.

Tucker got Marge's point and corrected her ma'am. "Marge. A thank you is more than enough, Marge. We all love Jace. And I keep telling Tyler, the garage is more than a place to work. It's a family. He's part of it now."

"I'm sure that goes over well, Tucker," Marge snorted.

Tucker laughed. "Yeah, about as good as you'd imagine."

"Having dealt with Tyler all these years, it doesn't take too much of an imagination." Marge grew serious. "I wish there was something more I could do to thank you for taking care of both our boys. Not being able to step in and take Jace was so hard, but knowing that Tyler and Jace are surrounded by kindness helps."

Mr. Matthews came out from the house and Marge waved him over. "Bill, this is Tyler's Angelina, though rumor has it, she prefers being called Tucker."

"Tucker, it's so nice to meet you." And with that proclamation, Mr. Matthews enveloped her in a huge bear hug. "My Marge has been beside herself worrying about our boys, but Ty's been telling us all about you, it's *Angelina this* and *Angel that.* You don't know how good it is knowing he's got friends who've stood by him. People who can see what an amazing man he is." Mr. Matthews choked up.

"Bill," Marge said, her eyes watery.

Tucker couldn't figure out why they were both on the verge of tears, but she knew she was missing something. Something big. For the life of her, she couldn't figure out how to ask.

Mr. Matthews continued. "All those so-called friends from the firm he worked with were quick to walk away from Tyler, like they stayed away when Jason was dealing with Mellie's illness. Fair-weather friends aren't worth the—"

"Bill," Marge said, her voice stern. "That will be enough."

"Sorry." He tried to look contrite, but Tucker could see true anger in his eyes. He was furious at the people who'd let Tyler down. And she got that—so was she.

"It's no problem," she assured Marge. "I work with a shop full of men, Mr. Matthews. I doubt you could say anything that would shock me."

"Oh, don't say that," Marge warned, her voice light as she very obviously tried to steer the conversation to less weighty matters. "Bill will take it as a personal challenge to try and come up with something to shock you."

Tucker chuckled and allowed the conversation to flow into calmer waters, but she couldn't help but wonder what she was missing.

Tyler Martinez was a man of secrets, but she felt some relief that even if he wouldn't share those secrets with her, he obviously trusted the Matthews with them.

He didn't think they were family, but now, more than ever, she was sure they were.

TYLER STOOD AT THE KITCHEN window and watched Angelina juggling Jace on one hip while captivating the Matthews.

He had no doubt they'd like her, and not only for what she'd done for Jace. There was something about Angelina that drew people to her, like butterflies circling a flower.

Thinking about butterflies made him remember her pink t-shirt and smile.

"Earth calling Tyler," Bart called.

"Sorry, I was thinking." He turned around and looked at Tucker's son.

"You were thinking about Mom, yeah, I know." Bart was so like his mother, if not in looks, then in attitude. Brash and to the point.

"I was thinking about other things."

Bart laughed. "Not buying it. Whenever you think about her, you get that weird expression on your face. But hey, don't be embarrassed, she gets the same sort of look when she's thinking about you. And I won't tell her you were staring out the window at her."

"I was checking on Jace." There, that was plausible.

Bart laughed harder. "Sure, you tell yourself whatever you need to, to get you through the day."

"Are you two bringing those burgers out? Lou is starting to get that hungry look," George said.

201

"I was teasing Tyler about Mom, Pops. Sorry."

"You can tease him while we cook these burgers if you like," George said amicably. "I'll even help you."

"Thanks, Pops."

Tyler rolled his eyes. "Oh, yeah, thanks, but really, Bart doesn't seem to need any help on that front. He seems to have teasing down to a science." And Tyler couldn't decide if he liked it because it made him feel like one of the gang, or if he didn't because it was another indication of how close he was becoming with the entire Tucker clan.

George obviously didn't have a problem deciding how he felt about Bart teasing Tyler. He laughed as he took the burgers out toward the grill.

"The Tuckers are a family as adept at teasing as they are at car repair," Bart said in a way that led Tyler to believe this was a conversation the three Tuckers had been in before. "Yeah, with all these talents, it's amazing we're all single isn't it?"

"Woman troubles?" Tyler asked.

Bart nodded. "You'd think being a friend would make being something easier. It doesn't."

Tyler felt like throwing up his hands and joining the chorus on that sentiment, but instead went for a safer, "People who don't realize what a catch the Tuckers are, miss out."

"Oh, people realize it about Mom. Guys are always trying to pin her down. Why, that Gary guy called again last night."

"Who's this?" Tyler asked, an uncomfortable possessive feeling roiling in his chest. He knew that he had no claims on Angelina. He kept telling her as much, but unfortunately, no one was telling him and every minute he was with her, he fell deeper and deeper.

"Some creep that Mom went out with a couple times. He's not taking no for an answer very well." Bart looked fierce. "She's been telling him no for a couple months now. If he shows up at the house, I'll be the one telling him no." Bart grabbed the condiments and followed his grandfather outside. Tyler mulled over this man who wouldn't take no from Angelina.

He wanted to find this guy and make sure he knew that Angelina was off limits. Not that he'd stand in her way when she was ready to move on to a man who deserved her. It was simply that this Gary guy obviously didn't deserve her at all.

"What's this Gary's last name?" he asked when Bart returned.

"Johnson. Gary Johnson," Bart told him. "But you don't have to look so worried. Mom can handle him. She's got experience."

"There's been other guys who won't take no for an answer?"

"Guys like Mom," Bart says. "Sometimes she doesn't notice. She thinks they're buddies. These guys tend to be guys she's not interested in long.

And some tend to be guys who don't take *no* well."

Tyler felt that old familiar rage build up in him like a long lost friend. He'd learned that kind of anger at his father's hand. Most of the time he could control it, but he suspected it would be hard, if not impossible, to control it with a guy who bothered or hurt Angelina.

He might not be the kind of man she needed, but even he was better than a guy who wouldn't take no for an answer.

"You okay, Ty?" Bart asked.

Tyler pushed back the anger that was the only true legacy his father had left him and nodded. "Fine. I don't like to see your mom have to deal with guys like that."

"She'll be okay. If he gets too pushy, we're all here."

"Good. I'll keep an eye on her, too."

Tyler tamped his anger as he cooked the burgers. It was easier than normal to bury it when the yard was filled with happy chatter. Jace raced from one person to the next, basking in their attention.

And in their love, Tyler realized. Every person at this picnic loved the kid.

Losing your parents at such a young age was hard, but Jace was surrounded by love. Not only his grandparents and Tyler, but everyone here. All the guys at the shop as well as the entire Tucker family. But especially Angelina. She lit up when Jace crawled on her lap, and so did Jace.

Tyler knew how the baby felt. He felt something inside him light up whenever she came into a room.

The Matthews seemed taken with her—with everyone from the garage—and as the evening wore down, they took Jace in for his bath, leaving Tyler to see everyone off.

Angelina was the last to go.

She stood out in the deepening evening and smiled. "I was right, you know."

"About what?"

"Hmm, it's hard to pinpoint one thing over another, I mean, I'm right so often. But this time, I was specifically talking about being right about the Matthews. They're your family."

"Angelina, don't—"

"I know, I know." She deepened her voice in a horrible attempt to impersonate him. "Don't push, Angelina. Don't prod. Don't ask uncomfortable questions about certified letters, or God forbid, don't talk about feelings. And don't discuss relationships and family. Not with Lone-wolf Tyler Martinez."

"Angel." He wasn't sure what he meant by that—by just her name. But she obviously figured it out because she stepped into his arms and kissed him.

"And don't read too much into sex, Angel," she whispered in her mock-Tyler voice between their kisses. "Soon, it will be over and you'll find the man you're meant to have. The man you deserve." She paused. "That's what you were thinking, isn't it?"

"It's like you have ESP," he admitted.

She shook her head, sending her short curls flying. "No, it's like you're a broken record. I've learned where you skip."

"Everything you said in my mock-voice was true."

"Doesn't make it right."

"Angel..."

"You live in the past, Tyler." Her voice was soft, and rather sad. "You worry that somehow your father's cruelty and drinking problems are contagious. They're not."

"That's not what studies say."

She snorted. "Studies? They're all wrong. At least about you. They speak in generalities, and Tyler Martinez is unique."

She stood on tiptoe and kissed him chastely on his cheek. "I should go now. Your family's inside waiting for you."

"The Matthews leave on Sunday." He meant to stop there, but instead found himself asking, "Maybe we could get together?"

"Are you asking me for a date? I mean, rumor has it I could do better." She laughed as she repeated his words.

"Rumor's right, in this instance. And better means someone better than that Johnson guy who's been hassling you."

Angelina nodded, her expression serious. "Okay, I'm going to admit that you're right, Tyler."

"Really? About what?" he asked suspiciously because beneath her serious expression he could spot a smile lurking.

"You're right that I could do better. Oh, so much better, Tyler. But at this moment in time, I don't want to. I can't think of anywhere I'd rather be than in your arms. So yes, I'd love to go out with you. Bet we can talk Bart into babysitting while I revel in your mediocrity for an evening?"

"How come even when you admit I'm right and I should feel like I won an argument, I still feel as if I'm a loser?"

"You are, but hey, when you take me on that date, we'll see if you can get luckier. I mean, really lucky."

Whatever cloud had darkened her mood earlier had blown over. If getting teased was the price he had to pay for pulling her out of her funk, he was willing to pay and play along. She hefted a mock-sigh. "Angel, I don't know what I'm going to do with you."

"The question isn't what you're going to do, it's what you want to do. What do you want to do with me, Tyler?"

His mind raced with all the many and varied things he wanted to do with Angelina Tucker. Unfortunately, he had the Matthews inside, so his desires would have to wait. "Ask me that question again after our date."

She laughed. "I will. Oh, you can bet I will."

TUCKER WENT INTO the office on Sunday morning. She was too revved up about tonight's date to sleep.

It was ridiculous, and she knew it.

She was a grown woman with a son who was leaving for college in a few weeks, and she was acting like a teenager.

She let herself into the building's back door and started toward her office.

There was a light on.

She considered there might be someone trying to break in, but if she were a thief, she'd steal expensive garage equipment. There was nothing in her office worth stealing. So she opened her door, and found her father sitting at her desk, staring at her computer screen with his reading glasses perched at the end of his nose.

"Pops?"

He looked up from the screen. "You're up early, Angel."

"Uh, so are you." She walked over to the desk and peeked at the computer monitor. "So what are you doing?"

"Checking the books," her father said casually, as if coming into her office and double-checking her work was a normal, everyday occurrence.

"Why?"

Her father didn't answer.

"Because you don't trust me?"

His expression said he thought she was being ridiculous. "Trust you? Certainly, I trust you. I wouldn't have stepped aside if I didn't trust you, but..."

She didn't need a psychology degree to know what this was about. "It's that Tyler's helping, right?"

"Right."

"You don't think I have enough business savvy to check his work?" She trusted him, on some deep level, despite all the evidence saying she shouldn't. But despite that innate confidence in him, as a matter of good business principles, she double-checked his work. After all, the garage wasn't only her livelihood. A lot of people relied on it.

Her father looked puzzled. "If you're checking it, then why have him help?"

How to explain to her father what she hardly understood herself. "First off, you can see how much more efficient his system is. It's all on the computer, Pops, and once everything's up and running, it should really streamline the paperwork, and that works well for me, and for the business."

She walked around the desk and sat down. "Secondly, I asked him to help because this is where he belongs. In an office. He's a great mechanic, but he's an even better businessman. He should be in an office, dealing with customers. Lou agrees. He's had Tyler doing more and more of the customer interactions in the garage." She paused.

Her father nodded and filled in, "And thirdly, you care about him."

"Maybe," was all she'd admit to her father, but in her heart she knew there was no maybe about it. She cared about Tyler Martinez. And her feelings were growing stronger daily.

"He's not what I wanted for you," her father admitted with a sigh.

"I don't think I'd sweat it, Pops. I don't think I'm what he wants—at least not long term. But hey, short term is better than not at all."

"You're worth more than settling, Angel."

"And you're biased, Pops. And unless you want me to start offering you advice with Marilyn, I'm thinking you should let me handle my personal relationship with Tyler."

"He was convicted of a crime," he said, as if it were news.

"Yeah? Well, I was a teen mother. That *was* part is what matters. I'm more than a teen mother now, and he's more than his conviction. I don't know why he did what he did, but Pops, I know Tyler. There was a reason. And someday, maybe, he'll share it with me."

Her father sighed. "So, if we're not going to advise each other on our dating lives, then I think it's time I broach the idea of a business partner again."

"Pops, I've got things under control. You've looked at the books, and despite a precarious economy, we're not only holding our own, we're growing."

"Your painting clientele is growing. That's where you need to concentrate. Maybe it's time Tucker's Garage added to its name. Tucker's Garage and Design. Or Tucker's Garage and Bodywork. But no matter what it's called, let me sell at least some of my share. Someone who would have a vested interest in the company. Someone who likes doing the business portion as much as you like doing the bodywork."

"Pops, it's way too early on a Sunday morning to start this fight. I'm not willing to bring some stranger into the garage as a partner. Even if I keep controlling interest. If you were to tell me Lou wanted to buy in..."

"He doesn't," her father said sadly. "I think he hates the business end of things more than you do. And he's thinking of retiring in a few years."

"And the other guys don't have enough money to make that move. And let's face it, Joe and North are young. I'd love to keep them with us for years, but there's a chance they'll move on. As for Tyler, you get nervous having him work on the accounts, I can't imagine you wanting to sell your stake to him."

Her father frowned. "So, we're at an impasse."

"Looks like."

He shook his head. "We could fight some more about it."

"We could, but managing your stress is part of the reason you've retired. I guess I look at it like this, Pops—you either trust me or you don't."

"I trust you," he said quickly, without hesitation.

"Then you're going to have to put this talk about a partner aside, because I won't agree. Oh, you could try to force the issue—"

"I've never forced you to do anything."

She'd known that and was glad of it. "Then we *are* definitely at that impasse."

"So what do we do?" he asked.

"I suggest that we head over to my house and I'll make some pancakes."

"You're going to feed me pancakes?" His surprise was evident. Since he'd been sick, she'd been very strict about his diet.

Tucker laughed. "Sure. I found this new recipe that uses whole grains and all kinds of other healthy things."

"You wouldn't mess with your grandmother's pancake recipe, would you? Is nothing sacrosanct to you, daughter?"

She glanced over her shoulder at the computer before shutting her office door and continuing her pancake battle with her father. It was easier to argue about pancakes than to argue about potential partnerships or Tyler.

Her father wanted more for her than Tyler Martinez, a man who'd told her in no uncertain terms whatever they had wasn't going to have a future. A man who was honest to the core.

And maybe that's why his whole embezzlement charge bothered her so much, because Tyler was honest to the core.

And honest men didn't steal money from their companies. They didn't embezzle from clients and do whatever they had to in order to hide the crime.

And, Tyler had never said what he needed the money for. He lived a cushy lifestyle, but given his job, she didn't think he lived beyond his means. He drove very nice cars, but he'd never owned more than one. He wore fancy, designer suits, but so did everyone else in his office, if what they wore to Jason's funeral was any indication.

So, why embezzle?

Maybe that's what she should ask him.

She wasn't sure he'd tell her.

Tyler was honest...when he said something. But he seemed as happy not to say anything at all.

And that was getting old, very, very fast.

CHAPTER NINE

TUCKER HAD GONE ON MANY first dates over the years. They'd ranged from boring, to uncomfortable, to nice-enough. She occasionally went out with the nice-enough guys again, but never the boring or uncomfortable ones.

When she thought about it, Tyler was her longest relationship ever.

She grinned and decided not to mention that to him. He'd read too much into it and start his lecture about her capability to do better.

"Wow, Mom," Bart said as she entered the living room.

She did a twirl then asked, "I look okay then?" The moment the question was out of her mouth, she realized how lame it was to require reassurance from her son.

He didn't seem to notice the lameness as he answered, "More than okay..." then qualified, "for a mom."

"Damned by faint praise."

He laughed. "More than okay for about anyone."

She felt better. "Well, that's nicer."

"Hey, do you mind if Cessy comes over tonight while I babysit?"

"You've been spending quite a bit of time with Cessy Keller lately."

"We've been friends for a long time. Since Aunt Eli and Zac got together."

"Yes, you have. But…"

"Maybe we're something more than friends now."

The admission cost him—Tucker could see it. Although she didn't know what to say. *Way to go,* sounded wrong, and being too pleased with his choice of girls would be misconstrued as lame, too. "Ahh…"

"It's not easy," he said quietly. "You'd think it should be. I mean, we're friends and all. But it isn't. And there's college coming up in a few weeks."

"Yes, college."

"Being at separate schools would make seeing each other hard." He shook his head, as if trying to talk himself out of it. "It's a bad time for us to become exclusive."

"But—" she started.

"Yeah, but."

Tucker slapped a hand on his shoulder. "I'd like to say that things will get easier, but that's a lie. Relationships are always complicated."

"How do you know if a relationship is worth the complications?"

"You'll know when it's right." She paused. "As for Cessy coming over, as long as her parents know you two are babysitting, I'm fine with that. To be honest, it's a great idea having the two of you babysit. Kids are hard and if you do decide that a deeper relationship with Cessy is worth the complications, I don't want it to get even more complicated by an unplanned pregnancy."

Bart shook his head with a look somewhere between annoyance and amusement. "Mom, not again, I think I'm old enough to do without your little life lessons."

"You'll never be that old, Bart. And let's face it, this isn't a little lesson, but a big one. A baby changes everything." She took his cheeks between her hands and made sure he was paying attention to her. She needed him to hear this. "I want you to understand that I don't regret a single thing about having you so young. My life's been enriched by you being in it. But I'm the exception. I had family to back me up. I had your Aunt Eli. I was so lucky. Not everyone is, though. And I want you to have a kid as wonderful as you are someday, but not now. So, don't rush things, okay? And if you decide at some point—and I'm not talking about Cessy here—but when you make that decision, make sure you're careful."

"Mom," he all but wailed. "I know about condoms and safe sex. We've had that discussion before, too." Then he muttered, "No one else ever had life lessons like you insist on sharing with me."

She shrugged and grinned as she mussed his hair. "What can I say? My life lessons are another way I say I love you."

He grinned. "And that's the only reason they don't drive me completely insane. And as for Cessy, could we not mention this to the Kellers, specifically Aunt Eli, yet? We're still figuring things out and you know, they'd all feel the need to have a say about it."

"Sure," she agreed.

"So where are you and Tyler going?"

Tucker shrugged. "No idea. Eli and Laura said this was a good choice for a no-idea-where-I'm-going-on-a-date outfit." She glanced down at the crisp, dark blue jeans and the pink strappy top which Eli declared was cute and feminine, without going overboard.

"Well, you look nice...for a mom," Bart said again.

As if on cue, the doorbell rang. Tucker hurried and let Tyler and Jace in. "Uck," Jace cried and threw himself from Tyler's arms into Tucker's, relying on her to catch him.

He hugged her for a moment, then spotted Bart coming into the entryway and squirmed to get down.

"I hope you don't mind, but I told Bart he could have Cessy Keller over while he babysits. They're flirting with the idea of something more than friends, but I don't think that will get in the way of him caring for Jace."

Tyler smiled. "If you're okay with it, then I'm okay."

"Thanks. I figure spending a night with an active baby slash toddler is a good way to remind kids to slow down and be careful."

"A life lesson?" She must have looked puzzled because he clarified, "Bart told me of your penchant for sharing your *wisdom*." That last word was punctuated by a smothered laugh.

"I'll have you know I'm wise. I'm very wise. Right, Bart?" she called.

"Right what?" he asked as he wrestled with Jace on the floor.

"I'm wise," she repeated.

"Wise ass maybe?" He laughed, then assured her, "You're very wise, Mom. And I'm smart enough to listen to your wisdom."

"Thank you. Now, you call if you have any trouble, okay?"

"I'll call. And Pops is at his place, too. But Jace and I are old buddies. We'll be fine."

"Don't forget what I said about Cessy," she added for good measure.

He sighed his teenaged my-mom's-going-to-lecture-me-to-death sigh. "I won't."

"Good." She leaned down and kissed his forehead, lost in the knowledge that in a matter of weeks, she'd be driving him to Pittsburgh and moving him into his dorm. She kissed Jace as well and couldn't help but remember when Bart was his size.

"Penny for your thoughts," Tyler used what was quickly becoming their phrase as they drove north on I-90.

"They're worth more than a penny," she assured him, but she didn't elaborate on what she was thinking. She was thinking that she hadn't been this excited about a first date in— well, ever. She was thinking about Bart, Cessy and new relationships. And she was thinking or rather wondering if he'd noticed she'd gone through another torturous round of Eli assisting her dress for him. She glanced across the car at him, and immediately thought that she wished they were back at his place and she could kiss him. More than kiss him, she wished she could strip him naked and have her way with him.

Yeah, all those thoughts were definitely worth more than a penny.

Tyler didn't seem to notice how many thoughts were chasing each other around and around in her head. "For our first official date I thought maybe we'd go into Erie for dinner then a walk on the beach at sunset?"

"That sounds lovely, Tyler." Not as lovely as he'd be naked in bed, but still, lovely.

"We would have had this date a couple years back if you'd accepted any one of my many invitations. I told you I'd wear you down eventually, but when I said it, I didn't know it would take this long."

Tucker knew that she could have had a couple extra years of friends-with-benefitting

Tyler Martinez and felt a spurt of regret. "But who knows what would have happened then," she said more for her own sake than his. "I mean, we've both grown and changed over the last few years. I love the man you are now, but it's impossible to know if I'd have loved the man you were then."

She realized what a stupid choice of phrase she'd used. "I didn't mean that the way it sounded."

TYLER SMOTHERED HIS quick spurt of disappointment. Of course, he didn't want Angelina to feel about him the way he knew he felt about her. He felt like a broken record thinking it, but it was the truth—she deserved more.

This date was a mistake. He'd known it all day, and he'd been telling himself as much, but like so many things regarding Angelina Tucker, he hadn't been able to resist.

He forced a laugh and said, "Obviously, you didn't mean you love me. And you're right, we've both changed since then."

The only constant in life is change. He should get that tattooed, a la North, as a reminder. Neither he, nor Angelina were the same people they were back then. He had her in the here and now, but soon that would change and when it did, he'd adapt.

Somehow they muddled through their dinner, what had once been so comfortable and easy, was suddenly strained and awkward. Tyler wished he hadn't mentioned the beach, but he had, so after their meal, they drove partway down the thirteen mile stretch of the peninsula, and parked near the Stull Center's building.

They walked to the beach in silence.

Not silence exactly. Presque Isle State Park was filled with people in the summer. It was alive with sounds and activity. People talking, walking dogs, music playing, cars driving by.

The noises helped mask the silence between him and Angelina.

They found a vacant picnic table and sat down. The sun still had a bit to go before it sank behind the water.

"Not the date you'd hoped for," he finally said. He realized he should be happy the date had tanked. It might make not having a second easier. Well, easier for Angelina.

"Even if there was a bit of eerie silence," she started admitting what he'd already known, "I'd still rather have a date like that with you than a perfect date with anyone else. I guess that's the problem."

He didn't have a clue what she was talking about. "That doesn't make sense."

"Oh, I know that. And I think I have a T-shirt that says as much."

"Of course you do." It was a joke that fell as flat as the rest of the date had, but he laughed obligingly.

She paused, as if considering her words and finally said, "When you asked me out before, well, I knew we wouldn't suit. We were too different."

"Designer suits versus jeans," he said, remembering this conversation.

Angelina nodded. "More than that, though. You were worried about appearances. The best suits, the best cars. Now, not so much. That was the point I was trying to make before. That first man, I wouldn't have wanted to date him for anything more than a physical attraction. Now?" She paused again.

Tyler knew that talking about things like this didn't come any easier to Angelina than it came to him. "It's okay. We don't have to—"

"It's not okay. I want you to understand. You're not the same man. When I first saw your house, I was surprised. It wasn't what I expected—what I'd envisioned you living in. And I don't think it's a house you would have considered a couple years back. You've changed. And I've changed. Somehow over the last two years, we've grown into people that do fit. Two people who share the same values."

"Values?" He'd never thought of his values. He had some. He didn't lie. He worked hard.

"Family first," Angelina said. "Care for others. Help when you can. Work hard. Enjoy life..." She rattled off a list she'd obviously been thinking about. "We fit. And you're still going to walk away soon. You regretted asking me out tonight—"

"Not regretted. I don't regret anything to do with you, Tucker." He purposefully didn't call her Angelina, and it was apparent she recognized that fact.

"But you had second thoughts," she maintained.

"Because I care about you."

She moved her hand forefinger to thumb. "Blah, blah, blah. I know this particular speech. And as nice as tonight's been, I'm going to agree with you."

"About?"

"Us. Bart leaves for school soon. I really need to spend some time with him, helping him shop and pack for his dorm. And with school starting, you should be able to find somewhere for Jace in town. I've never been one for stretching a relationship beyond what it is. I think we've stretched this one as far as we should."

Tyler knew he should be happy. This was what he wanted for her, and yet her words hurt. "As a matter of fact, I think I have a sitter. A Mrs. Kovalski. Mrs. Keller suggested her. She's had her neighbor's children during the summer, but with them going back to school, she's interested in meeting with me and Jace. She'd be able to start with him in a week at my house if we fit. I think the continuity of being home would be a good thing."

She was quiet a moment, then nodded. "You're right. Having a continuity of care in the same house is probably a good thing. No more juggling." She smiled, and maybe someone else would buy it, but Tyler knew her better. She was putting on a brave face as she nodded again and said, "One week then. You'll have Jace's care taken care of, I'll be getting ready to send Bart off to school and we'll be over."

"So, this is our one and only date?"

"I think we'll both agree that's best. With Bart gone, for the first time in my life, I'll be on my own and can try to figure out who I am, and what I want. I want to be a little selfish for a while, and tying myself down with a man and a baby would make that hard." She kissed his cheek. "But thank you for a lovely...interlude."

Tyler forced a smile. "It has been great, Tucker. I think it's what we both needed, but you're right, it's time to get on with our real lives." He took her hand in his. It was a sturdy hand that knew all about hard work, and it fit surprisingly well in his.

He dropped it. "So, could I interest you in a short walk down the beach. If this is our one and only date, I'd like to do it right?" he asked, trying to ignore the feeling of desolation that swept over him as he thought about ending things with Angelina. He knew it was the right thing, that her father was right, she deserved better than him,

224

but that didn't make it easier to turn around and walk away from the best thing that ever happened to him.

"What you're suggesting is that we make the most of the night?"

"Yes." If this was going to end, then he wanted the rest of tonight to be perfect.

"And how about the rest of the week?" she asked. "I mean, we'll still be juggling Jace's care, so I'll be seeing you a lot more than the average employer sees an employee..."

He should say no. After tonight, they'd go their separate ways, well as separate as they could go and still work at the same shop. But he knew he didn't want to say goodbye, at least not quite yet.

"One week from today we're done and our little—" he deliberately used a word he knew would minimize what they had "—fling is over."

"As if it never happened," she agreed, nodding.

That decided, Tyler knew he wanted to make the most of this week. He wanted to savor every minute, because he knew he'd never find anyone else like Angelina Tucker.

THIS WAS NOT THE WAY Tucker had imagined the evening. She'd all but broken up with Tyler— well, pre-broke up. In a week they'd be done.

She'd walked away from men in the past, she could do it again. But she had a reprieve and she was going to revel in it. "Bart's planning on spending the night at Pops' after we go back to your place and get Jace. They're planning a very early morning fishing trip. He didn't want to wake me," she told Tyler as they strolled down the shoreline.

They walked along the water's edge on the firm, wet sand that was speckled with small stones and bits of tiny mollusk shells. Seagulls perched on the large stone breakwalls that helped stem the beach's erosion. The sun sank closer and closer to the horizon, where the lake met the sky.

"Bart's spending the night at your father's?" Tyler asked.

"You know what that means?" she prompted.

"No."

"I don't have a curfew. And since we've decided that this," she waved her hand between them, "is over in a week, I think we should make the most of it."

"What do you suggest?"

"I suggest you say, *Tucker, spend the night with me. The whole night with me. Let me make it the most memorable night in your life.*" She tried to infuse the sentence with the right touch of light, flippant humor, although she felt anything but light and flippant.

Tyler let out a long, low whistle. "Wow, that's a tall order."

He was trying to keep things as light as she was. "I know from experience that you're *up* to the task."

He groaned. "That was bad. Really bad."

"Yeah, but ask the question."

"Tucker, would you spend the night with me? The whole night. I'll try and make it the most memorable night of your life." He managed to keep the question light and teasing, despite the decision they'd reached. This is what Tyler wanted. What he'd said since the beginning. Nothing long term. Nothing deep and meaningful.

Tucker didn't blame him. His life was in upheaval. He'd lost his friend, he'd inherited a baby and he'd lost his job and his identity.

No, she couldn't blame him.

"Yes," she said. "We'll make it a night to remember."

It wasn't his fault that she'd gone ahead and fallen head over heels in love with him.

CHAPTER TEN

ON WEDNESDAY, TYLER was struck with an overwhelming realization as he arrived at work. Something that he wouldn't have believed before life, as he'd known it, had fallen apart.

He liked being here at Tucker's Garage.

The fact that he'd see Angelina every day was part of it, but not all of it. He simply genuinely liked the work.

If someone had asked him before everything happened, he'd have said he never wanted to do car repairs again. He'd had his fill of mufflers and oil changes growing up. He'd accepted being a mechanic out of desperation. He needed a job and no one else wanted to hire a convicted thief.

When George Tucker had offered him a chance, Tyler expected to punch in each day, do his time, then punch out. He assumed the actual job would be a grind and that he'd hate it.

Yet, as he walked into the garage today, he looked forward to it, found a certain peace here despite occasionally having to listen to the noise of air hammer and impact gun. He liked the feeling of accomplishment when he figured out what was wrong with a vehicle, then fixed it. He even liked the faint smell of exhaust and oil that seemed to permeate garages, no matter how good the ventilation system.

Tyler almost laughed at the thought as he digested this new insight.

When he was young, and his father was too drunk to repair a car, Tyler had done it and he'd resented it. A twelve-year-old shouldn't be responsible for putting food on the table. When Tyler couldn't figure out a problem, or what to do about it, he'd haul his old man's sorry ass out of bed and make him show him.

He'd hated it. Hated every minute. Hated missing classes to do a repair. Hated the ever-present oil under his fingernails.

But now?

He smiled as Joe and Lou teased North about his new girlfriend. He'd been with Jen since the Fourth of July outing. And they were going strong, which meant the teasing at the shop was even stronger.

"Come on guys," North said, "she didn't dress like Star Trek characters or Star Wars. She dressed as Sookie Stackhouse."

"Who?" the other two guys asked.

North shook his head in disgust. "A girl who dates vampires in a book series and on a television show. I know old men don't follow popular culture, but it's a big show. Vampires are a huge trend."

"Vampires?" Joe asked. "Come on, North, aliens and starships aren't enough, now you're dating a vampire?"

North grimaced. "Jen's not a vampire and neither is Sookie. Sookie's part fairy, but mainly human."

"Oh man..." Lou said.

Tyler laughed and the guys turned around.

"You gonna weigh in, Ty?" Lou called.

Joe nodded. "The kid's dating a vampire..."

"She only dressed like a girl who dates vampires for a convention," North protested.

"Yeah, that's right, she's half fairy," Joe's tone was serious, but his expression was anything but.

"I'm not getting into this," Tyler said, laughing. "I know when it's best to stand back and let you guys go at it." He left his three colleagues arguing about vampires and went to check the worklist. As he listened to Lou and Joe giving North a hard time, he was struck all over again by the realization that he liked it here.

He was good at his job, and he loved coming here each day.

That was something.

He was beginning to understand how important that was.

Angelina appeared with Jace on her hip. And Tyler realized it wasn't only Lou, Joe and North that he liked working with.

"Just checking in with everyone," she called to them with a smile. "Jace and I are heading to my office to make some calls."

"Poor Tucker," North called out. "It has to be torture to call people and be all nice and accommodating." He glanced at Lou and Joe, apparently hoping they'd join in and tease Angelina, but the two of them simply waved at her and started back to their work stations.

"Hey, at least it's not paperwork," Tyler said as she walked by him and he chucked Jace on the chin.

Angelina groaned. "No, the paperwork comes after the calls."

Tyler laughed. "I could take care of some of it for you this afternoon. I think Lou's giving me a light load so I can help you."

"I should go yell at him and assure him I don't need to be coddled, but instead..." She left the sentence hanging, ran over and hugged the very confused senior mechanic, and winked at Tyler as she took Jace back to her office.

Only a few more days and Jace wouldn't be coming in with him.

And he and Angelina would call whatever-it-was-they-had quits.

Somehow he'd adjust because that was what was best for Angelina. Bart would be gone and for the first time she'd be on her own. Solo. Independent. Able to do anything and everything she hadn't been able to do with a child at home.

He'd miss her, but he'd find a way to live with it because it was the right thing to do. He loved her enough to want her to have more than a felon.

Some of his happier mood faded.

He knew that dating Angelina would be selfish, but that didn't keep him from wishing things were different. He, more than most, knew that a man's name meant everything, and he'd seen to it his name meant as little, or less than his father's had.

He went to work and tried to ignore his rapidly darkening mood.

An hour later, North called, "Hey, Ty, phone!"

Tyler crawled out from under the Smart Car he'd been working on and wiped his hands on a rag as he walked over to the phone. He picked up the receiver. "Hello?"

"Tyler, it's Henry Rizzo."

Tyler's happy mood when he came into work wasn't just darker, it shattered. "Yes, Henry? Is there a problem? I've done everything I was required to do according to my parole officer."

His attorney was silent a moment and then asked, "You've got a few letters lately, right?"

Tyler thought about Angelina's finding the most recent one. Certified this time. "Yes. I've got them. But my understanding was, I'm not legally required to meet with them."

"You read them, the letters? You realize this could be major?"

"No," he said. "Uh, I read the first one, and I'm not interested, so I've tossed the others."

"Not interested in being exonerated? In having the court clear your name, without any prodding on my part, without my filing a motion?"

He thought of Angelina and wished he could give another answer. If his conviction was wiped, as if it never happened, maybe they could...he could... He shook his head. Mrs. Matthews used to say if wishes were horses even beggars would ride. When the Matthews took him in, he'd admitted that sometimes wishes did come true. He had a family, albeit a borrowed one. He'd been granted a wish. But as an adult he was aware, lightning didn't strike twice.

He knew that if he exonerated himself, Jason would pay the price, and through osmosis, Jace.

Tyler knew what it was like to grow up with a father whose mere name was an embarrassment. He wanted more than that for Jace. He couldn't live with himself if he saved his name at Jason's and Jace's expense, so he said, "Yes, Henry, I'm sure that I don't want to pursue this. That is exactly what I'm saying."

"And I'm saying the judge and ADA requested a meeting with you informally over lunch on Friday. They asked me to call you and strongly encourage you to be there."

"I don't want to go."

"Listen, Tyler. I'm your attorney and I can't imagine many instances where I would tell a client to meet with an ADA and the judge who sentenced them, but I've talked to Jackie, the ADA, numerous times since this all came out. And I think you should meet with them."

"They're not going to change my mind."

"Then look on it as a chance to convince them of that. However, as your attorney, I'm going to suggest you rethink your position. Carrying around a record is tough. Carrying one around when you didn't commit the crime and could have been exonerated? That's asinine. You could have your old life back."

Angelina came into view outside the garage with Jace in her arms. Jace squirmed and she set him down and he sprinted to North, who scooped him up and twirled the baby a little too vigorously for Angelina's liking. She walked over to them and scolded, while North and Jace both laughed. Pretty soon Joe and Lou joined the group and Jace jumped from person to person, a small dictator with his minions willing to do his bidding.

They all loved him.

He was part of their family.

And Tyler realized that despite himself, so was he.

"Tyler?" Henry said. "You still there."

"Yeah. And I heard you. I could have my old life back. But you're wrong, I can't go back. I think we both know that."

"Then you could build a new life, one with a clear name."

That was something different. If clearing his name would have made him the man for Angelina, he might have agreed, but even then— he looked at Jace so happy—he wouldn't do it. The price was too high. "I—"

"You only have to meet with them Friday," Henry interrupted. "Noon, lunch at that restaurant in the Convention Center's hotel."

"If I meet with them, that will be it? They'll back off?"

"Yes. I can see to it that they do."

Tyler sighed. "Fine. I'll meet with them on Friday."

"You won't regret it, Tyler," Henry said. "I'll meet you there."

"No, Henry. I don't need an attorney for this. I'll show up and tell them thank you, but no thanks. I'm not doing it."

"I've only been involved in criminal cases for a few years, Tyler. And I've had a lot of different clients. Some who were innocent. Some who weren't. I had one person who readily admitted she was guilty of the charges, but claimed she was an accidental arsonist. Carly's the one who made me rethink my career as a contract lawyer and switch to criminal law. And I think I've made a difference. But with all the guilty and the innocent people I've repped, I've never had one who was innocent and was happy letting the world think he was guilty."

"You know why—"

"I know what you've said," Henry said. "But I think you're wrong. Everyone in question thinks you're wrong."

"But you're tied by attorney-client privilege, right?"

"Right," Henry assured him, punctuating his response with a heavy sigh. "But go to lunch on Friday and hear them out."

Tyler agreed and hung up the phone. He knew he'd do it all over again. But for a while, he missed his old life. He missed the name he'd built for himself. Now...

Now, he had a new life. He had friends who'd already shown they'd stick by him no matter what. Family.

It was a heady feeling.

As Jace came into his arms, Tyler acknowledged it was a feeling he would never give up.

Later that day, he talked to Lou about extending his lunch hour long enough on Friday to get into Erie and go to a meeting, promising to make up the time. "I wouldn't ask if it wasn't important."

"I know that. You go, we've got Jace covered."

"Thanks."

"No problem. It's going to be kinda lonely when he starts in with that sitter next week." Lou sounded wistful. "The younger guys don't remember what it was like when Tucker had

Bart, but I do. Having Jace around reminds me of that. You should have seen Tucker then. She was just a kid herself, but she was an amazing mom. She put that kid first from the minute she found out about him."

Tyler nodded, not the least bit surprised. "That sounds like her."

"She's not someone who's quick to share herself, but when she gives her heart, she doesn't hold anything back. She gives herself completely. None of us would ever want to see her hurt. And if you're in trouble again, she'll be crushed." Lou's look was full of dire warning.

"No, I'm not in trouble. Nothing like that." Then without thinking, he added, "I'd never do anything to hurt An—Tucker if I could help it."

Somehow calling her Tucker made him feel more distant—and distance was what he needed. He'd get the new efficient systems up and running, and then with Jace safely placed with a sitter, he'd hardly have to do more than wave to An—Tucker each day.

"I'd never hurt her," he reiterated.

Lou nodded. "So, that's the way of it. I'm not surprised. She's a special lady."

"Too special for me," Tyler assured him. "And she knows it."

Lou's expression said he didn't quite believe it. He studied Tyler, and finally nodded. "All right, then. But it's not only you being in trouble that will break her heart..." Neither of them needed him to say more.

"And I'd never want that to happen. That's why Tucker," he congratulated himself for not even hesitating over her name this time, "and I have always been very clear about the nature of our friendship and the fact that it can never be anything more."

"I think you're both fooling yourselves, but who am I to have an opinion on it? As long as she isn't hurt, you and me, we're square. As for Friday, we've got you covered here."

"Thanks, Lou. I'm going to go check it out with Angelina, too." Damn. "Tucker," he corrected.

"Sure. You check with her, kid." Lou shot him a knowing smile that Tyler chose to ignore as he walked down the hall to Angelina's office. The door was ajar, and she was talking. He peeked in and saw she was addressing Jace, who was playing with some blocks in the middle of the floor.

"...and then I said, no way. He's the most annoying man I ever dated."

He knocked and stepped in, ready to defend himself against her claims. "Who's the most annoying man?" He knew he should hope she'd say him, but he found himself taking umbrage at the thought.

"Gary Johnson."

"The guy who won't take no for an answer? What did he do now?"

"Oh, get that look off your face. My honor doesn't require defending. Anyway, I'm quite capable of defending myself. Something Gary Johnson is now intimately aware of."

"What did you do?" Tyler asked.

"I told him in no uncertain terms that the only way I'd ever go out with him again would involve the end of civilization as we know it, the demise of every other male, and it would still probably require my own personal lobotomy to make me say yes."

Tyler found himself grinning at her very vivid description. "I take it he got the picture?"

"Sadly, no." She shook her head in disgust. "But then I reminded him that my friend Laura has a husband who's a cop and I would actively pursue a restraining order if he bothered me again. And I'd be sure his employer got a copy."

"Ouch." He knelt down by Jace, who obligingly shared a block with him.

She nodded. "Yeah, I think he finally got the picture then."

She seemed confident, but Tyler still didn't like it. "If he gives you any other trouble..." He left the threat hanging.

Rather than appreciating his concern, Angelina grimaced. "Thanks, but I don't need you, or anyone else, rescuing me. I'm not looking for a white knight, I'm looking for a partner."

"That's not what I hear." He put another block on top of the other, making a two block tower, which Jace promptly swatted, then cackled with glee as it fell into ruin.

"I was referring to a partner in life," Angelina said, "not a partner here at the business. You've been talking to Pops?"

"No, but in case you missed it, the guys in the shop gossip like women in..."

Angelina's scowl told him he'd be hard-pressed to find an analogy that wouldn't offend, so he simply backtracked and said, "Gossip like a magazine about the newest celebrity craze."

"Nice save," she said.

"Thanks. I didn't come back here to gossip or trade quips. I wanted to be sure it was all right if I took a long lunch on Friday. Lou said it was, but I don't want you to think I'm taking advantage of our...friendship. I need to take this meeting."

"If Lou said okay, it's okay with me. He's pretty much taken over the scheduling in there, although he hates it as much as I hate this..." she waved at her computer screen.

"Can I do anything?"

"No." He made another two block tower, which Jace immediately knocked down and chortled over. He kissed the baby's head. "I should probably get used to dealing with things on my own. You and your dad rescued me with this job, and then with Jace. I need to take care of this solo."

He started for the door, but she called him back. "Tyler. Is everything okay?"

"You mean about the meeting?"

She nodded.

"It's an annoyance, nothing more serious." He tried to give her his most reassuring face and wasn't sure she bought it.

"If you need anything, you let me...all of us, know."

"I will."

He started toward the door again, but turned back. "Want to come over to my place after work?" Since they'd decided that this week was it, he wanted to make the most of every minute with her still.

"Yes. I got a new t-shirt I can debut for you."

He groaned. "You look way too happy about it. I think I'm nervous."

He managed to get all the way out of her office this time, the sound of her laughter ringing in his years.

Tonight, he'd make a memory that he could hang onto when his time with Tucker was over.

And somehow on Friday, he'd convince the judge and ADA to drop the talk of clearing his record, then return to this new life he was building for himself.

The only way he'd like this new life better was if he kept Angelina in it, but doing that would be selfish. She mocked him when he said it, but it was true...she deserved more than he could give.

But for tonight, he was going to give her everything he could.

TUCKER PARKED IN TYLER'S driveway and went to the backdoor instead of the front. She realized that next week, she'd probably revert to being a front door guest. The thought brought down her happy mood, so she immediately pushed it aside.

Live in the now.

That was her mantra for tonight. And right now, she going to spend time with Tyler and Jace.

Bart said he had plans with his grandfather for the evening, so she didn't even need to feel guilty about skipping out on one of their last mother-son nights together.

"Tyler?" she called as she pushed open the screen door and walked into the farm kitchen.

"Don't come up here. I'll be right down," he called.

Curious, she thought and wondered what he was up to.

He came back with Jace in one hand, and an overflowing diaper bag in the other. "You made it."

"I said I would." She took the baby from him and Jace promptly hugged her. In that moment, Tucker totally melted. As she held the toddler tight. He smelled of a bath, of baby soap and lotion. "You bathed him this early?"

"He's got a date of his own tonight," Tyler said.

"Oh, I figured he was staying with us."

"You figured wrong."

As if on cue, a car horn beeped. From the back door Tucker saw her father's truck with Bart riding shotgun.

"They're taking Jace for a while."

"What did you do to make my father agree to that?"

Tyler smiled cryptically as he took the baby from her and walked out to the truck.

Tucker let the three guys load Jace's carseat and watched as her father and son drove away with Jace, leaving her alone with Tyler.

"So, it's only the two of us," she said.

"Yes, and..." He stopped and looked at her shirt which proudly proclaimed, *Date—it's a 4 letter word. Come to think of it, so are the words high and heel.* It showed a woman tilting on stilettos.

Tucker assured him, "I wore it just for you."

He laughed and so did she.

"Bart got it for me for Christmas one year. I guess I grumble a lot about putting on girl clothes and I'm pretty sure high heels were invented by a man. That's what I love," she corrected herself, "I've loved about my time with you. You don't seem to mind that I'm not a runway model. I've enjoyed our friends with benefits time." And though she wouldn't say the words, she knew she'd miss it when it was over.

She really hoped she could maintain a friendship with Tyler, but she knew it wouldn't be the same.

"Tucker, I don't mind a single thing about you." He pulled her into his arms and tenderly kissed the top of her forehead. It wasn't the least bit carnal, but simply sweet.

She could have stood like that, wrapped in Tyler, for a very long time. Too soon, he pulled back. "So, are you ready for our date."

"I sort of thought you'd be cooking dinner..." She jerked her head at the pristine kitchen. "Are we going out?"

"Out to the living room." He took her hand and pulled her down the hall and into...a fairyland.

He'd closed the drapes, strung small Christmasy lights everywhere, lit a small fire and had spread a blanket in front of it. There was a bottle of champagne chilling in a bucket and the coffee table was spread with an array of finger foods.

"How did you get all this done?" she asked.

"Lou let me leave a little early. I'll make up the time on Saturday for today and Friday."

"No one's ever..." She sniffed, determined not to cry.

"Angel?"

She'd noticed that he'd been calling her Tucker the last few days, and she figured it was his way of distancing himself, but tonight, he reverted to calling her Angel. It was too much. She felt a tear creep out, despite her blinking.

"Angel?" he repeated.

"No one's ever done anything like this for me."

"What. No one's ever been crazy enough to start a fire in the middle of summer, then crank on the air conditioner so you don't melt?"

"Don't," she said. "Don't minimize this. This is romantic. It's a sweet gesture, one no one else would do for me. Even though I'm wearing a goofy T-shirt, you have a way of making me feel as if I'm the most beautiful woman in the room." That sounded far too sappy to her, so she tried to play it off as a joke. "Of course, at the shop, I'm generally the only woman in the room, so I guess—"

"Don't," he told her. "Don't minimize yourself. Some women need to dress to the nines in order to create an illusion of beauty. You simply have to be you. It doesn't matter if you're wearing a weird T-shirt and holey jeans, or that pretty sundress you wore to the picnic. You're always beautiful."

Standing there in her T-shirt looking at all the trouble Tyler had gone to, Tucker truly felt beautiful. "Since you went to so much work getting ready for our dinner, maybe you wouldn't mind if I take care of the appetizer?" She slipped her T-shirt off and revealed her sexiest bra.

"I think this might be my favorite appetizer of all times," he said, accepting her gift.

As she made love to Tyler, she tried to ignore the thought that this was almost over.

For the first time in her life, Tucker wasn't ready to let go of a relationship that had run its course.

For the first time in her life, Tucker wasn't sure she'd ever be ready to let Tyler Martinez go.

CHAPTER ELEVEN

ON FRIDAY, FEELING RATHER like a man on his way to an appointment with a guillotine, Tyler hurried out of work an hour before his normal lunch break and stopped at home to change. He wasn't sure why this meeting felt so ominous to him. He wanted to get it over with as quickly as possible.

He thought about pulling out one of the two suits he'd kept after he lost his job. He'd gotten rid of everything else. The rest of the suits, his house, the car. He'd liquidated and paid the restitution and his legal fees, then banked the little bit that was left over.

He fingered one of the remaining suits, but he'd worn it to Jason's funeral and didn't want to put it back on. Plus putting on one of the suits from his former life might give the ADA and judge the wrong impression. He simply wanted to go to this lunch and tell them *no*. Then he could get back to the life he was building and leave the past behind him.

He settled for khakis and a polo shirt. Dressy enough to show respect for the judge, but nothing more.

247

Normally, he loved coming down to the dock in Erie. The city had worked hard to take the area from its industrial past into a city tourist hub. The Bicentennial Tower at the end of the dock was one of his favorite attractions. From its top observation deck he could take in the full scope of the bay as well as the peninsula across the water. Today, he barely registered it, or any of the other tourist attractions, as he made his way to the restaurant.

"I'm here to meet Judge Bradley," he told the hostess and noted his nervousness might have made him sound curt, so he tacked on a, "please," to try to soften his words. After all, it wasn't her fault he was forced to be here.

She smiled and picked up a menu. "Your party is waiting for you, sir."

She led him back to a table in a quiet corner of the restaurant. He recognized the judge and the young ADA from his trial.

The third person at the table turned and he realized it was Jason's dad, Bill Matthews. "Mr. Matthews? Why are you here? When did you get back in town?"

"Sit down, Tyler. You remember Judge Bradley, and ADA Kelley?"

He nodded. "Sir, Ma'am." He sat in the vacant chair and tried to figure out what Jason's father was doing here.

The judge cleared his throat. "I know it's unusual for a judge to invite a convicted felon and the ADA who prosecuted him to lunch—"

"Unusual has never stopped you before," the ADA muttered.

Other than his one trip to court, Tyler hadn't had any experience with the judicial system, but even he knew that probably wasn't the most appropriate way to speak to a judge, but the judge in question didn't seem to notice and continued talking as if the woman hadn't said a word.

"—but when ADA Kelley was telling me about the new information in your case, I'll confess, I was a bit confused. After talking to Mr. Matthews, I was even more confused by your stance." He paused, and leaned further toward the middle of the table and added, "And Mr. Martinez, I hate being confused. So I thought maybe you could explain it to us all over lunch."

"Explain what?" Tyler asked, desperately wishing he was anywhere but here.

The judge looked exasperated. "Explain why you don't want your name cleared."

Tyler hadn't expected such directness. "ADA Kelley—"

"You can call me Jackie, sir," she told him. "We're not in the courtroom and it's really creeping me out to have you all keep using my title and it's even worse when you ma'am me."

"So let's be informal and get right to the point," the judge said. "Tyler, did you embezzle that money?"

The waitress came to the table and asked if they wanted anything, which gave Tyler time to choose his words carefully before she left with their drink orders and he had to answer. "I took a plea, went to jail and paid restitution for the embezzlement, sir. Is that something an innocent man would do?"

Mr. Matthews patted his hand. "Son, they know everything. Jason talked to Jackie here before his accident and he confessed. Signed some papers to that effect. He urged her to reopen the investigation and gave her dates and times to validate his claim."

"And for the record, Mr. Martinez, I noticed that you didn't answer my question," the judge said in a stern voice. "Did you do it? It's not like we can legally do anything more to you if you admit it. You've served your time. Just a yes or no answer, if you please. Did you do it?"

When Tyler remained silent because he simply couldn't think of any way to wriggle an answer any more honestly, the judge continued, "I know what your friend said, though only through what ADA Kelley has told me about their meeting. And I know what Mr. Matthews here has claimed his son told him. But I didn't hear it from your friend directly, so I'd like to hear it from you. Did you embezzle money from your firm? Yes or no, Mr. Martinez?"

Tyler didn't respond.

"Tyler didn't do anything but be a good friend—a brother," Mr. Matthews said.

"And that, sir, is what I've been working with." The ADA's frustration was clear in her voice. "Like I said, Jason Matthews has confessed to the crime. I never felt particularly good about this case, but when you have someone taking a deal on a charge you take their plea at face value. But when Mr. Matthews came into the office and confessed, I pulled out our files and went through the evidence with a fine tooth comb. I'm not a handwriting expert, but I could see some discrepancies in some of the documents, so I had them tested. Our expert concluded the signatures in question were not Mr. Martinez's, but were far more likely Mr. Matthews's. Everything else that Mr. Matthews said checked out as well. I feel confident that we prosecuted the wrong man. Since Mr. Martinez isn't seeking exoneration, it would be easy for me to walk away, except for this tiny little worry about justice."

She turned to Tyler. "I took this job because I believe in the idea of justice and I have never lost any sleep about putting away a criminal, but I've lost sleep over this case because I truly believe I prosecuted the wrong man. That's not justice. That's not what I signed on for."

Judge Bradley nodded. "Mr. Martinez, I've reviewed ADA...Jackie's findings and I agree with her assessment. Mr. Matthews was a friend, I believe. I have a lot of friends, but I don't think I'd take the fall for one who did something so stupid."

"Tyler, you and I both know why Jason did what he did," Bill Matthews said. "And it was stupid. I understand Jason's desperation, but that doesn't make what he did right."

Tyler knew what his friend had done was stupid. He'd said as much the day he'd punched his friend. "Let me ask you, sir," he said to the judge, "what if you and your wife were told you were pregnant, after years of trying, and then the doctor said he'd found some irregularities in her bloodwork and wanted to do further tests? What if he came back and told you she had cancer, and the best option for your wife was aborting your miracle baby and starting a treatment that could save her life? And what if she refused to do it?" His throat tightened as he laid out Jason's story for the judge. He missed his friend so much.

His voice lowered as he continued, "What if you found some questionable therapy overseas that claimed to be able to hold her cancer at bay long enough for her to deliver and take more traditional therapies here in the states after the baby was born? What if you thought it was the only way to help save your wife? What if, in a moment of utter pain and confusion, you did something horrible and stole money, thinking you could pay it back before anyone noticed? What if you were wrong and they noticed?"

The judge nodded. "And what if your friend was accused and took the fall for you?" It was obvious that the judge had what-iffed more than that. "What if he pled no contest to the charges and hurried things along, to ensure the authorities didn't dig too deeply into the case?"

"That's not an admission on my part," Tyler stated. "We're playing what-if."

"Your friend's dead, Tyler." The judge's voice was soft, but Tyler winced at the bald statement. Jason was his brother, for all intents and purposes, and he wasn't sure he'd ever get used to a world without Jason in it. A world without Mellie.

As if sensing his thoughts, Mr. Matthews reached across the table and patted his hand.

"He's dead," the judge continued, "but he confessed before he passed. Jackie and I both believe him. Setting the record straight can't hurt your friend. Maybe it's the only thing that will truly allow the man to rest in peace."

"It's what Jason wanted," Mr. Matthews said.

"So, explain it to us. Why aren't you filing a motion and demanding that your name be cleared?" the judge finished.

Tyler didn't know how to make them understand. "A father's name should mean something. A son should be proud of his father."

The judge agreed. "And you don't think his son would be proud of a father who made a mistake, a foolish mistake prompted by love and pain, then did everything he could to rectify it?"

"What I know is what it's like to grow up ashamed of your father. Not being ashamed, but hating him. I don't want that for Jace."

"And you're raising the boy now, right?"

"My wife's barely recovered from her last surgery and needs another, we couldn't take the baby, so Tyler did." Mr. Matthews turned to Tyler. "You honored Jason's wishes in that regard, you're caring for his son. You need to honor his wishes in this, too. Let the judge and ADA clear your name, Ty. You can have your old life back. It's what Jason wanted."

Jackie said, "That baby's lucky because he has a biological father who was strong enough and ethical enough to confess to a moment of weakness, and he'll be raised by a man who would do anything for a friend."

"What if Jace doesn't understand what his father did? What if he hates him?" Tyler knew he was projecting his own feelings for his father onto Jace.

"Mr. Martinez," Jackie said. "I know I'm going to sound young and naive, but I really believe in my job. I believe that truth should win out. That justice should be served. And I don't believe that justice is always easy. You didn't commit this crime. You've been careful all along. You've never directly confessed to doing it. You've been honest, even if ambiguous, but sir, I know you didn't do it. Mr. Matthews confessed. His father here has been hounding my office to pursue justice in this case, and justice means clearing your name."

"Even if I don't want it?" he said to all three of them.

"Maybe especially if you don't want it," the judge said. "Everyone associated with this case has discussed the findings. ADA Kelley, myself, the police department, our forensic handwriting expert, and even your old boss at the firm. We're all agreed that you didn't do this, and while we could wend our way through the legal system to expunge your record, we've all decided on a different course. As of today, you're no longer on parole. We've had it terminated early. And I've already spoken to the governor, and ADA Kelley will be approaching him formally to request that he pardons you."

Tyler had never felt so frustrated. How could they still not get it? Images of his father lying on the kitchen floor where he'd collapsed in a drunken haze, waiting to be discovered by Tyler and a friend after school.

The cops bringing his dad home, or picking his dad up, while the entire neighborhood watched.

The time his father had broken his arm and forced him to lie to the sympathetic nurse at the hospital.

He knew what it was to have a father who did nothing but humiliate and embarrass. He would do anything for the baby.

Anything.

He needed to make them all understand. "I don't want—"

The judge interrupted him. "We're not negotiating this, Mr. Martinez. The wheels are already in motion. When you're cleared, you'll be able to apply for your license again. You could have your investment job back."

Tyler hadn't even considered that possibility. "I don't know what to say to make you all understand."

Mr. Matthews patted his shoulder. "There's not much to say other than thank you, son."

"But—"

"But nothing," the judge said, sternly. "Our job isn't simply to prosecute and judge, our job is to serve justice. Both Jackie and I, and everyone else involved in this case, agree that your name should be cleared. It's what justice demands." He took his napkin off the table and placed it on his lap with flourish, as if to indicate the formal part of their discussion had ended. "So does everyone know what they want for lunch?"

"I need to leave," Tyler said, and walked away from the table without even saying goodbye to Mr. Matthews. He walked out of the restaurant feeling shell-shocked.

They said he could have his life back. Maybe they were wrong. The governor might refuse to sign the pardon. But the judge and the ADA didn't sound like it.

He followed the sidewalk to the dock and stared out at the smooth water of Erie's bay.

He could have his life back.

His condo, his cars.

Designer suits on a daily basis.

He could rewind the clock. How many people got to do that?

He should be thrilled.

And yet he wasn't.

Free and clear.

He could try to return to the firm, but the other day he'd realized how much he loved the garage. He left his house every day with a sense of anticipation. He asked himself how he'd felt each morning heading into the firm, as opposed to how he felt heading into the garage.

He was happy at the garage. He loved the guys he worked with. And they were right, they'd made him feel like part of the family.

He bought a ticket and went to the top of the Bicentennial Tower, which rose from the end of the dock and looked out over the bay. Rather than taking in the picturesque sights, his mind continued going in circles. He had no idea how he should feel, or how he actually felt.

"Son?"

He turned and found Jason's father behind him. "Mind if I have a seat?"

Tyler nodded at the bench and asked the question that had been bothering him since he showed up at lunch and found Mr. Matthews there. "Why?"

"Why what?" Jason's father asked.

"Why were you there, encouraging me to let them ruin Jason's name? He's your son. You should want to preserve his memory."

"He's my son and he made a mistake. A terrible mistake. I'm proud that he owned up and that he tried to make things right."

"Make things right at the expense of his son."

"You really think that Jason's admitting what he did will make Jace think less of him?"

Tyler nodded. "How could Jace not be affected? I mean, I don't plan to say anything about it, but when he gets older, he could find out."

"He will find out because I'll tell him."

"Mr. Matthews." Tyler's frustration mounted. Everything was changing, and he didn't know what to do or how to feel about those changes. He just knew he wanted to protect Jace.

Jason's father patted his shoulder. "I plan to tell my grandson about my two amazing sons. The one I raised from birth and the one who became part of our family later. Jace will never know his biological father, but he'll know you. He'll learn from you. Things like honesty, honor, friendship, loyalty...love."

Tyler didn't know how to handle compliments, so he snorted.

"As to how could I be with the ADA and judge this morning..." He slid closer to Tyler. "No matter what Jason did, I loved him and was proud of him. My definition of a man is one who makes a mistake and does what he can to fix it. The same goes for you. I was there today to support you because I love you. I've always been so proud of you. And I don't know how to put in words how I feel about what you did. You selflessly took the blame for what Jason did. You gave him the time to be home when Mellie needed him, to be at her side when she died. You did that selflessly because you loved him, and I would tell you to allow him to set things right. He would have been here today telling you all these things if he could. Since he can't, I was here to represent him."

"But what about Jace?"

"My grandson is blessed. He was born out of Jason and Mellie's love. And now he's surrounded by love. Ours, yours and all your friends at the garage. He's got two fathers whose names he can be proud of."

"Mr. Matthews..."

"Tell your friend Angelina the truth, Tyler. There's a very good chance this story will get picked up by some news outlet. A man who gave up everything to help a friend? The networks would be all over it. And even if it stays hush-hush, she should know the truth."

"Why? She's my boss, nothing more." Tyler knew the lie even as he uttered the words.

So did Mr. Matthews. He chuckled. "Wow, I thought you were a man who didn't lie. Either you're lying to me, or to yourself."

"Maybe I do care about her more than I should," he admitted, "but she deserves better than me."

"What she deserves is the truth, and between you and me, son, she could spend the rest of her life looking and she'd never find a man who held a candle to you. Ever. Your greatest gift is your ability to love wholeheartedly." He paused a moment and added, "And as long as I already have you riled up, I should mention I'm also here for the closing on Jason's house."

"It sold already? Good." He knew that was going to be one less problem for the Matthews. Right now, they needed to focus on getting Mrs. Matthews well.

"It sold and he has a nice little bit in equity," Mr. Matthews continued. "If you take that, and Jason's insurance money, there's enough to pay you back for what you paid in restitution."

"That's not necessary. The money is Jace's."

"There will still be enough to start a college fund for him."

"I don't want—"

"It's not open to negotiation, Tyler. Let Jason rest in peace knowing his debts here were settled. Well, not completely settled because no amount of money can pay you back for what you did for him, and what you're doing by taking care of Jace. I'm going to let you think this all over. Marge, she tells me that you're a muller. You need to work things out for yourself. So, work it out, and take the check from me graciously. Be happy, son. That's all we want for you."

He left before Tyler could say anything else.

Mrs. Matthews was right and Tyler knew it. He was a muller. And he knew he had so much to think about, to figure out, he could sit here and mull a long time, but he needed to get back to work. He'd mull some more tonight, after he'd put Jace to bed.

Unless Angelina was there with him. Then he'd have better things to do than mull.

Tell her, Mr. Matthews had said.

Be happy, he said.

Tyler's greatest gift was to love? He scoffed at the notion. He needed to think, to try to figure out what he should do. What would be best.

He went back to work and everyone there seemed to sense he needed time with his thoughts. Even North steered clear.

After work, Tyler walked to Angelina's to get Jace. He stopped at her screen door, entranced by the scene inside.

"Jacie poo, Tucker loves you," Angelina sang.

Bart groaned. "Mom, seriously, don't call the kid Jacie, or worse, Jacie-poo. No boy can survive being known as Jacie-poo in school. He'll get beat up and picked on and—"

"Do you really think the name Jacie-poo will stick until he's in school?" she asked with a laugh.

"Bart did," her son said dryly.

"Point taken," she said. "I should feel bad about that, but you are definitely a Bart, not a Spencer..."

The two of them continued their banter as Angelina stirred something on the stove with one hand, and held Jace with the other.

Jace was content being held by Angelina.

Tyler had noticed how the baby's face lit up every morning when he saw her. He flat out ran to her and expected to be picked up immediately. Jace loved her.

As he had the thought, Angelina leaned down and nonchalantly kissed the baby's head.

She loved him.

And Tyler loved them both. For the first time, he wondered if he and Angelina could have a chance. Should he tell her and let her decide? Should he take a chance?

Could he take a chance that he could become the man she deserved? That they could become a family? The ghost of his father settled over him, and he remembered what Angelina had said about seeing himself through his father's filter.

He'd never hurt Jace, or Angelina. He could almost believe it. He knew he'd never want to, but what if in a moment of anger he forgot?

Partway through another verse of her Jacie-poo song, Angelina spotted him. "Tyler, what's wrong?"

"I was coming to get Jace, but I wonder, if instead, you could keep him a little longer. I really need—"

He didn't even finish the sentence and Angelina said, "He's fine with us for as long as you need. Overnight if you'd like. Go ahead, it's no problem."

That was it. No questions. No recriminations. Just her trust and willingness to help.

Tyler had planned on turning around and going, but first, he opened the screen door and kissed her. Kissed her because he knew he loved her.

Bart made a gagging noise in the background and Jace, in Angelina's arms, tugged on Tyler's hair and still he kissed her.

When they finally broke apart, she asked, "What was that for?"

"I'll tell you later." And he rushed out.

He still had some thinking to do, but in his heart, he knew he'd already answered the most important question.

"SORRY THAT OUR GIRLS' night out has become a girls' and kids' night out," Tucker said as Eli and Laura arrived, kids in tow. "Bart said he'd stay home with Jace, but it's his last weekend in town and I know babysitting wasn't what he had in mind."

"No problem," Eli said. "Zac was almost beside himself at the thought of a quiet solo evening. He swore he was going to do nothing until I got home."

"Sounds kind of boring to me," Tucker admitted.

"No, I'm with him," Eli said. "I love the kids and all the noise that comes with them, but sometimes, I crave the silence. Zac took them out for lunch a few weeks ago, and I sat home and simply lost myself in the silence."

Tucker realized that after Bart left next week and Jace started going to the new babysitter, she'd have plenty of silence. The thought didn't sound quite as nice to her as it obviously did to Eli.

"Poor Seth is on second shift tonight. So he won't get to enjoy any silence," Laura said. "I had to promise Jamie's grandparents that they can have him tomorrow. And Seth's off. Oh, whatever shall we do?" She grinned as she asked the mock question.

Tucker smiled as they took all the kids to the backyard and the small wading pool she'd bought and filled with buckets and water toys.

They sat and talked, catching up on each other's week. Jace played with Eli's two kids and Laura's one.

Tucker kept up with the conversation, but Eli's off-the-cuff comment on silence ate at her. She was losing Bart and Jace, and she'd agreed to walk away from whatever her relationship was with Tyler and begin a strictly friendly employer-employee one.

She deserved more.

That was her father's and Tyler's refrain.

When Bart was little she'd dreamed of the faraway day when he'd go off on his own and she could finally be on her own.

Now, with sudden insight, she knew that being on her own meant being alone and that in this case it meant being lonely.

She listened to her two friends talk about their lives, their families, their husbands, and despite what she'd always told herself, Tucker knew that's what she wanted. A partner. Someone she belonged to. Someone she belonged *with*.

Not simply an abstract someone, but specifically, Tyler.

She didn't want their relationship to end next week...or ever. But he did. She felt morose and hung her head slightly.

Enough to force herself to look at her T-shirt.

One Foot on the Accelerator...

On the back she knew it read, *One Foot on the Brake.*

It showed a woman in a convertible, her hair flowing in the wind behind her as she drove.

Tucker's short strands would never flow, but she was in control. She had her one foot on the accelerator, the other on the brake. She could decide which to press.

Because Tyler said brake, didn't mean she had to listen.

She was in control.

She didn't need to accept her father's or Tyler's dictates. She didn't have to live by what she'd thought she should want. She could decide what she did want.

She didn't need to think it over, she knew. She'd known for a long time. What she wanted was Tyler and Jace.

The only question was, how did she go about getting them short of beating Tyler's hardheadedness? "Eli and Laura, I need some advice."

Her friends stopped their conversation and waited for her to continue. "Tyler thinks our relationship ends this weekend because I deserve the best, and he doesn't think that's him. But while I agree I deserve the best, I know the best man for me is Tyler. So what do I do?"

Eli sighed. "The Tucker I've always known is a strong, independent woman who has never let anyone dictate what she should and shouldn't do."

"And she's kind," Laura added. "She's the type of person who will help you even when you say you don't want help. She'll show up in a snowstorm with only a sweatshirt on to bring you food. She's an amazing woman."

"Who's raised an amazing son," Eli said. "She doesn't let anyone dictate to her."

"You think that's what I'm doing with Tyler?" she asked, though she knew the answer.

"Well, you've admitted you want him," Eli said. "But seem willing to give your relationship up because he's said so."

Laura picked up the tag-team dialogue. "What you need to ask yourself is—"

She didn't let her friend finish. "What I need to ask myself is, do I want Tyler enough to fight for him? Especially because the person I will be fighting is Tyler himself?"

Her friends both nodded.

"So, what are you going to do?" Eli asked.

"I'm going to lull him into a false sense of security," she said, realizing she'd made a decision. She would fight for Tyler.

"I'm going to let him think I've given up as quietly as he wants. I'll take next week off and spend it with Bart, getting ready for, then moving him into college. But once he's settled, all bets are off. Tyler will have thought he won, but I'll sneak up on him and I'll make Tyler Martinez realize he can't walk away from what we have, much less walk away from me."

Tucker studied her two friends. Eli, who'd been a part of her life for going on twenty years, and Laura, who was a more recent friend. And she suddenly knew that even if she didn't win her battle with Tyler's stubbornness, she'd never be alone.

Neither Laura or Eli mentioned Tyler's past. They didn't tell her that she could do better. They simply dove in and helped her make her plans.

She thought of a T-shirt Eli had given her a few years back. Friends Are Like Funeral Homes...Both Will Help You Bury the Body.

THE FOLLOWING THURSDAY evening, Tucker surveyed her truck. "Okay, that's it." She was impressed they'd managed to fit all Bart's things in it.

She thought of Tyler. Not because packing a truck in any way reminded her of him, but

267

because no matter what she'd done all week, she'd thought of him. She wasn't sure what to make of him. She thought after they broke up, he'd steer clear of her, but instead, he'd been friendly and even asked how Bart was doing. Mainly he kept giving her the oddest looks. As if he were thinking or plotting something.

Or maybe that was her guilty conscience projecting on him, because she was certainly plotting and planning ways to convince Tyler he was the man she deserved. The only man she wanted.

He had turned over the new accounting and invoice system to her on Sunday. It was definitely going to cut the paperwork down, but not down far enough as far as Tucker was concerned.

Tyler seemed okay with the end of their relationship. She'd left Sunday night hoping he'd say don't. Stay. Though knowing he probably wouldn't. He didn't disappoint. He'd let her go, and she'd simply gone.

"So, let's go say goodbye to Jace and Tyler," Bart said, pulling her back to the present.

She looked at her son. Having a child when she was not much more than a child herself was hard, but somehow they'd managed. In some ways, they'd grown up together. She reached out and touched his stubbled cheek, which served as a reminder that he wasn't her little boy any longer.

If she were another kind of woman, she'd probably sniffle a bit, but she knew Bart would hate that, so she chucked his chin instead and said, "Yeah, they're waiting to say goodbye to you."

Bart motioned toward the packed truck. "We should have packed the Pilot after we went over. I would have been easier to drive."

"Yeah, driving it packed to the brim is a bit of a pain. So, maybe, instead of driving my Pilot, we'll take your car."

Bart's head snapped in her direction. "My car?"

She reached in her pocket and took out a set of keys and nodded at the gold Blazer sitting in the back of the garage. "It's geriatric, but another way to put that is it's a classic. It's got four-wheel drive and the motor's in great shape. You can work on the body during school breaks. Pops and I thought it would be a great incentive for you to come home."

He hugged her. "Mom, I don't need any incentive other than seeing you all, but really..." He squeezed harder. "Thanks. I didn't have a clue."

"We all wanted to surprise you. And rumor has it, there's a certain girl in your life who might be glad you have some wheels."

Bart scooped her into a giant hug. "Thanks, Mom. I mean, really..."

She felt her eyes fill with tears that she'd never shed. "We own a garage. This was nothing."

"Can I run and find Pops before we go? Maybe he wants to drive over with us. He misses Jace, too."

Before she had a chance to say go, he ran behind the garage toward her father's. She smiled. That worked out well and his having a car meant that he'd have a way to come home on weekends, at least at first. She imagined that once he got to school and settled, his visits home would be infrequent at best, but she suspected his visits to Cessy Keller's campus might be more frequent.

And that was the way it should be.

Bart was ready to start a new chapter, and once she'd settled him, so was she. She was going to make Tyler Martinez see that he couldn't live without her.

She'd played all her possible moves over and over in her mind all week. She was running through them again when Bart ran back. "Pops can't go, Mom. He's waiting for Marilyn."

"Then it's the two of us. Let's go."

He crawled into the driver's side of the car and checked out the panel. "This is sweet, Mom."

"Two rules before you officially own it. You'll never drive without seatbelts, and you'll never drive if you've been drinking...anything. Even one drink. You have to promise."

He raised his hand in a boyscout sign. "I swear, Mom."

"Good." She sat back and watched him grin as he drove the short distance to Tyler's. He was out in the backyard with Jace as they approached. He'd put in a sandbox, she realized, and felt out of sorts that she'd missed out on that. Not only did she want a real relationship with Tyler, she wanted to be part of Jace's life, too. She'd thought that she might revel in her soon-to-be childless state; instead, she wanted to jump right back into it. She wanted Jace and Tyler. A package deal.

"Hey, shrimp," Bart called as he got out of the car and scooped up the baby. "I'm going to miss you."

Jace squealed as Bart twirled him around. Tucker stood against the Blazer, noting the scene and feeling as if her heart would explode. Even thinking that made her feel way too sentimental, but there it was. Her baby was grown and leaving soon.

"So, how are you holding up?" Tyler asked as he approached.

"Good. I mean, I'm going to miss him, but I have plans. I've never had to make decisions for only myself before. Everything I did had to have Bart's welfare first and foremost."

"Now, you need to think about yourself." Tyler nodded, as if he agreed.

"Yes. I'm going to do exactly what I want, when I want."

His laughter didn't quite reach his eyes. "All I ever wanted was your happiness, Tucker." Then he switched the subject from her happiness to Bart's. "Did he like the car?"

"Yes. More than like. I suspect he'll be home a number of weekends working on it."

"That was nice." They both looked across the lawn where Bart was handing the baby off to an older lady.

Tucker liked Mrs. Kovalski. And it was apparent that Jace did as well. Tucker knew that having Jace cared for in his own home had been a priority for Tyler. He wanted the little boy to have that security. She turned back to Tyler and said, "Well, when your mother owns a garage, you probably should have your own car. I could have gotten him something nicer, but I don't believe in giving people things. He should have to work for it, too."

"Our econ teacher loved to say there's no such thing as a free lunch."

"Exactly." She directed her attention to Mrs. Kovalski and Jace. "So, how's she doing with him?"

"Great. And how is the new program working in the office?"

"Really good. Although if I have a problem with it, I'll holler. I mean, you're down the hall most of the day." Just down the hall, in the main garage, but it felt like a million miles without their having to run back and forth, talking about

Jace, trading off duties. "We should probably be going."

"Thanks for bringing him over."

"No problem. We're leaving first thing tomorrow for Pittsburgh. I won't be in the office at all, but Pops will check in and I'm sure you and Lou can handle anything else that comes up."

"I'm sure we can."

"Bart?" she called.

He sprinted over to them.

Tyler extended his hand as he said, "Thanks for all the help with Jace, Bart. Thanks for everything. You know if you ever need something, you only have to call."

Bart shook Tyler's hand, so grown up. "No problem. Jace and I are buddies, I can't wait for him to get older. We'll do lots of stuff together." Bart smiled warmly. "I'll see you soon. I've got a lot of body work to do on the Blazer."

Tyler looked past Bart and caught Tucker's eye as they shared a smile. Bart turned and walked toward the car.

"Bye, Tyler," Tucker said softly as she followed her son.

"See you, Tyler," Bart called as they pulled away.

Tucker glanced over her shoulder as they pulled onto the street.

"Are you really going to let him go, Mom?" Bart asked.

"Pardon?"

Bart concentrated on his driving, staring straight forward, not at her as he said, "I've noticed that he hasn't been over this week. After spending the summer together, you've suddenly cooled things off. I'm not asking whose decision it was, but I'm going to say that you shouldn't let him go. At least without a fight."

Her son was much more observant than she'd have thought. "I'm not going to. I'm lulling him into a false sense of security. He thinks he's won and that I'm letting him go because I realize I *deserve better.* What he doesn't realize is I have no doubts about what I deserve. He doesn't realize that he's the best, and that's what I'm going after. Once I get you to school, I'll show him."

"He's not going to know what hit him," Bart said, laughing. Then sobering up, he said, "Really, Mom, you should be happy. I want to say thank you."

She patted the ancient car's dashboard. "Yeah, it was a great surprise. I think it was a better surprise than the year I got you the mini bike."

"It was, but really, I want to thank you for everything. I can't imagine having a baby at my age. Jace did make me understand how difficult it must have been for you. Yet, despite your age, you were the best mom ever. All my friends always wanted to come to my house because you were so cool. I never once doubted you loved me or that you supported me. I..." He shrugged.

"Before I leave for college, I wanted you to know that I know how hard you worked. That, and I love you."

Tucker felt an uncharacteristic dampness gather under her eyes. "Oh, man, you're going all mushy on me. Waxing nostalgic and all that," she joked, then more seriously added, "but for the record, you're welcome. Being a mother at such a young age wasn't easy, but you were worth all the effort and every moment of it. You're an amazing kid and you're growing into an amazing man. I'm so proud of you."

"Mom..."

She shook her head and waved her hand between them. "Enough of the mushy stuff. By my reckoning we won't be required to go down this lane again until your graduation, then maybe at your wedding and... Well, milestones. We'll make a date to be mushy during milestones, but the rest of the time, we're just us."

He laughed. "Deal."

"So, drop me off at home and go have some fun on your last night here. Don't forget, we're out of here first thing in the morning, and you'll be driving, too, so get in early enough that you can manage it."

"I will."

She stood outside the shop and watched Bart drive away. She thought about going into the house, but it would be too quiet and she wasn't up for that. So, she let herself into the garage instead. She'd get some work done so that it didn't pile up while she was gone.

And as she got ready to paint, she thought about her upcoming showdown with Tyler Martinez. He was right. She deserved the best. Somehow she was going to have to convince him that while he was right about that, he'd overlooked the fact that he was the best for her.

She didn't think they made a T-shirt for that.

CHAPTER TWELVE

AT THE END OF THE NEXT day, Tyler had Mrs. Kovalski drop Jace off at the shop for him. He had the baby settled on his hip as he walked across the lawn to George Tucker's and knocked on the door.

"Hey, Jace," Angelina's father said as he opened the screen door and scooped the baby into his arms. "Come on in, Tyler. What's up? You need me to watch Jace?"

"No. Well, yes, but not now. Now, I'd like to talk to you."

George went to the kitchen table and sat down, indicating the other chair across from him. "Sounds serious."

"It is," Tyler assured him as he took the seat.

George handed Jace a spoon and the baby happily beat the table as George said, "Shoot."

Tyler had spent the better part of the week mulling. He'd talked to Mr. Matthews again and had finally acknowledged there was nothing he could do to stop the ADA from clearing his name. He looked at Jace and part of him still worried about the baby. He wanted to be sure that Jace understood what his father had done and why.

If Mellie and Jason had done anything differently, then Jace might not be here, Mr. Matthews had said. In my book, that makes them both brave. Doesn't negate Jason's mistake, but it does make him human. And maybe that's what Jace will need. A father who was brave and human.

Somehow, Tyler would see to it that Jace understood it all. That he knew about his father, mistakes included.

"I don't want to get into specifics yet, Mr. Tucker, but you hired me when everyone else ignored me. You gave me a chance to rebuild my life. And now, my name is going to be cl...cleared." He stumbled over the words. "I'm not sure how I feel about that, but it is what it is. I have a chance to go back to my old life, or..."

"Or?" George asked as he gently guided Jace's spoon back to the table top and away from his face. When Tyler didn't answer immediately, George repeated, "Or..."

"Well, I want to talk to you about that."

An hour and a half later, Tyler left George Tucker's house and he had a plan.

TUCKER GENERALLY AWOKE on Mondays with optimism. The upcoming week was a blank slate. It could be something amazing.

She stared at the tank of the Sportster she was hoping to finish today.

Saying goodbye to Bart on Friday had been tougher than she'd imagined, but she'd talked to him yesterday and he was having a great time. The orientation weekend had been fun, he'd assured her. Knowing that made letting go easier. She'd spent the last eighteen years preparing for this day. The fact that it had arrived and he was adjusting wonderfully meant she'd done her job right.

She knew that her relationship with Bart would change. He'd grow up, move out and find a life for himself.

She simply hadn't expected the rest of her life to be in upheaval as well.

"Hey, honey, I talked to Bart last night," her father said as a way of announcing himself.

She set the spray gun down and turned around to face her father. "I'm glad he called you. He sounded good, didn't he?" She climbed to her feet and smiled.

"Yes, he did," her father agreed. Then abruptly he said, "I wanted to talk to you about my selling off some of my shares."

Her mind was full of Tyler, about how she was going to approach him and confront him. The last thing she wanted was to pick up this fight again. She'd thought after their last discussion her father had given up. "Pops—"

"No," he held out a hand, "hear me out. I have an investor in mind and all I want you to do is meet the person. It would do my heart good to know you at least gave this a listen. You have the final say, but Angel, I think this could be a match made in heaven. Everything I wanted for you, and maybe everything you wanted, even if you didn't know you wanted it," he finished cryptically.

"Pops, *It'll do my heart good?* That was pretty low. And I'm sure that I know exactly what I want and a partner isn't it." Her father simply waited, not responding, and Tucker sighed. "If I meet with the investor and say no, you'll back off? Not just back off, but drop the subject entirely?"

He visibly relaxed. "Yes."

"Fine," she said, feeling like a wimp for caving.

Her father smiled and said, "After work then?"

"I had plans after work today." Plans that involved Tyler. She still hadn't come to any actual concrete plans other than showing up on his doorstep and saying *I love you,* then outlining why his past and her past didn't matter—only their future did.

"Can you put your plans off until after the meeting?" her father asked. "It really is important, or else you know I wouldn't ask."

Tucker snorted. "Yes you would."

"Yeah, you're right. But we're on. Today, after work. He'll meet you in your office." Her father turned to leave her paint room.

"Pops, you didn't tell me who my mystery meeting is with."

"I know," was his cryptic response. "He'll be here at five."

TUCKER THOUGHT ABOUT changing before her meeting with her father's secret buyer, but opted not to. After all, whoever it was wanted to buy into the business. They shouldn't have some unrealistic idea about who she was.

She glanced down at today's green T-shirt that read, *Only the Wind is Allowed in My Face.* That definitely set the tone for the meeting.

She glanced at the clock. Five to five.

She opened up her computer, but knew she wasn't fooling anyone. She couldn't concentrate on the forms in front of her.

"Angelina."

Tucker saw Tyler in her doorway. His jeans were neatly pressed, and his workshirt was not only equally pressed, but also pristine, despite the fact he'd worked all day. Even now, without his high-powered business suits, he was as impeccable as ever.

Back when he'd asked her out—it seemed decades ago—she'd joked with Eli that he was designer suits and the only designer she knew was Jacqueline Smith at K-Mart. They were ill-suited both figuratively and literally.

And yet.

Tyler Martinez was a perfect fit for her.

He didn't think so, and she suspected it was going to take some serious negotiating on her part, but somehow she'd make him understand. But not now, with her mysterious potential partner coming in. "Ty, what's up?"

"I was hoping to talk to you."

She glanced at the clock. It was five on the dot. "I have a meeting in a few minutes. Can it wait?"

"No, I'd rather tell you now," he said.

"Come in and close the door then. We may have to cut this short, though. Pops's surprise should be here any moment. I could come over after my meeting?" They'd definitely have more privacy at his house than here. And even though she didn't have a specific script in mind, she knew what she wanted to say to Tyler should be said in privacy.

"If we're interrupted, I'll go. But I want to start now, before I lose my nerve."

Tucker scoffed. "Yeah, like that's going to happen." She pointed to the couch, and followed him over and sat on the other end. "You've never been someone prone to nervousness."

"This is different," he assured her.

She wanted to kick herself—or maybe kick him. She had so much to say to him, but not here. Not like this. For now, she'd listen. Later, she'd shake some sense into him. "So, talk."

"Do you remember that registered letter?"

"Why no, Tyler, it totally slipped my mine," she teased, but when he didn't laugh, she immediately quit doing so. "Yes."

"It was..." He shook his head. "Okay, let's start at the beginning. My father was a drunk. We've sort of covered this, but I want to say it all. I don't remember a time he didn't have a drink either in his hand, or close at hand."

"I'm sorry," Tucker said. "But you're nothing like him." She'd tried to reassure him of that before, but she didn't think he believed her.

"He was a mean drunk." Tyler continued. "And he was a mechanic when he was sober, but by the time I was twelve or thirteen, he was rarely sober enough to work, which meant he got fired from every garage he worked at. He started doing repairs out of the garage at home, *I ain't workin' for no one else ever again,* he told me, as if he had a choice, as if he'd been the one to walk away rather than the one fired. Problem was, he didn't do the work, so I took care of the cars at night. It kept us afloat."

"Oh, Tyler, I'm sorry." She prayed that whoever her father was sending over was late.

Tyler nodded. "Jason, Mellie and I were friends. Jason's family took me in. I lived with them my senior year. They're the ones who saw to it I went to college. We were all in college together. I was best man at their wedding. Jace's godfather..."

The story tumbled out. Mellie's illness, Jason's embezzling money from the firm to pay for her treatment.

"He thought he could pay it back before they found out. He was going to sell everything and..."

Suddenly it all made sense to Tucker. She'd been right, Tyler hadn't done what they'd said he'd done. "Before Jason could pay it back, they discovered what he'd done," she supplied.

"I was part of the team that found the discrepancies. And I was the one who figured out it was him. I went to him and when he confessed—"

"That's when you punched him." Everything. All the bits and pieces she'd learned about Tyler fell into place finally.

"I would have sold everything to pay for Mellie's treatment. If he'd come to me, we could have figured out an option that wasn't illegal."

"But he didn't, so..." She waited for Tyler to tell her what she already knew.

"I went to my boss that night and told them they should stop the investigation. It was gratifying that he didn't believe I did it. Not at first. He asked me point blank if I'd done it. I told him to call the cops. I told him I couldn't confess until the prosecution came up with a deal. But I assured him that I was willing to pay restitution."

"*Couldn't.* I'm sure you phrased it that way," Tucker said. "Couldn't confess, not wouldn't." Tyler nodded. "But your boss, he didn't catch it."

284

"No. He didn't catch it. And when the police came, I wouldn't talk to them, but I instructed my attorney to make a deal. I wouldn't contest charges, that I'd willingly pay all the money back and serve whatever time they thought fair with only one condition, that they proceed immediately. I wanted the case expedited. I wanted my conviction established."

"So they wouldn't look too closely at the evidence and realize what happened," Tucker continued.

"Mellie was dying." Even after all this time, Tyler tripped over the word. "She was the bravest woman I ever knew—willing to put off her own treatment for the baby's sake. She deserved to have her husband at her side. The baby deserved a father he could be proud of."

"And you? What did you deserve, Tyler?"

"No one expected me to make anything of myself. I was Deacon Martinez's kid. My fall from grace wasn't news to anyone...it was inevitable."

"So why are you telling me all this now?" Tucker asked.

"Mr. Matthews, the judge in my case, and the ADA are clearing my name. They think there's a chance I could have my old life back. My job—"

"The money and the cars?" It would all be his. He'd be back in his designer suits, living in some swank apartment. He'd leave Tucker's Garage in a New York minute, there was no doubt in Tucker's mind.

He'd leave the garage, and he'd leave her. Tucker didn't know what to say, so she simply said, "Congratulations, Tyler. You've been great here at the garage, but we both know you belong somewhere else."

"Where I belong, now that's a question," he said slowly. "It's why I'm here, talking to you."

"Sure it is." She wanted to scream. She felt so frustrated. Part of her wished she'd made her case to him first. Part of her was thankful that she hadn't made a fool of herself. "You know we wish you all the best. You don't have to worry about giving notice."

"I wasn't worried about giving you notice. You see, I have a proposition for you."

Tucker went from feeling devastated at the thought of losing Tyler to insulted in the space of a heartbeat. "Wait a minute, you think that if you get your old life back, I'd be interested in dating you? You told me I deserve better, and now that you'll have things the way they once were, you think that makes you better?"

"No." He reached across the couch and took her hand. "Although figuring out that I don't want it all back does."

She shook her head. "I don't understand."

"Everyone thinks the governor will pardon me. That I'll be totally exonerated, and able to get it all back. That's what the lunch was about a week ago. I've been thinking it over ever since. Mulling, Mrs. Matthews calls it."

"Mulling." Yeah, Tucker could see that. "So, what have you decided after a week's worth of mulling?"

"I don't want it back. Right before my lawyer called and told me I really needed to meet with the judge and ADA, I'd been thinking how much I enjoyed it here at the garage. I'd been good at my old job, but I'd never experienced much happiness while doing it. Here, I like it all. I like working on a car, and then standing back and realizing I'd done that—fixed it. I took something that was broken and made it better. It's tangible. And I like the people I work with. I'm happy here."

"So, now that your name is going to be cleared, you're going to do something that makes you happy?"

"I'm going to try. Although, it's not completely up to me."

"No?"

"It's up to you, Angel." He squeezed her hand, and before she could pull away, he gave a small tug, moving her closer to him on the couch. "I went to your father and asked if he'd consider selling me his part of the business. I'd like to be your partner."

"My business partner?" she repeated stupidly.

"Yes."

"Oh." She pulled her hand from his and felt even more stupid. She'd told herself that she was going to make him think she'd finally admitted that she did indeed deserve better. And she did. She deserved the best. And even before she'd heard his story, she knew Tyler Martinez was the best.

Of all the men she'd ever known, he was the only one she'd ever felt this way about.

She'd hoped that he was going to admit it himself—admit they belonged together.

The fact that he simply wanted a business partnership hurt, but it didn't change anything. She was going to fight for him—even if it meant fighting Tyler himself. If she were his business partner, she'd definitely have more time to win him over to the idea they belonged together on a permanent basis. "Really, my business partner?"

"If you'll have me. You'd own the controlling percentage and you'd also have a partner who likes doing the accounting end of things."

"Won't our previous relationship make things awkward?" she asked.

"Ah...about that. I know you deserve more than me. More than I can give you. But I'm hoping you'll give me the opportunity to grow into the man you deserve."

Tucker clued in to what he was saying and her heart lept. She tried to keep from smiling as she said, "No."

"No? You don't want to give me the opportunity?" He nodded, as if he'd expected it. Then his head jerked up. "I'm not backing down on this. I'll fight for you."

This time Tucker couldn't manage to hold back her grin. "Tyler, you are such a dork. You don't need to fight for me. You've already won. I simply meant I'm not waiting around for you to grow into a man you think I want when you're already exactly the man I want right now. A man who, when he gives himself, gives his whole heart. Look at what you did for Jason and Mellie. That's what I want. I don't want you lecturing me about who I should want. The kind of man I deserve. I want you. I want to come home to you every night. I want to build a family with you." She leaned across the couch and kissed him. "I want you to be my partner in the garage...and in life."

She kissed him again. This amazing man who had the biggest heart of anyone she'd ever met.

"I love you, Tyler Martinez."

"I love you, too, Angel."

EPILOGUE

SIX MONTHS LATER, TYLER found Angelina in her paint room. She was staring intently at a motorcycle's fuel tank, as if waiting for inspiration to strike.

He didn't need inspiration. He simply needed more luck. He felt almost greedy hoping for more, but there was something about Angelina that made him want to reach for more. To be more.

"I have a present for you," he said, extending the package toward her.

Tucker opened the bag. "Another T-shirt? Ty, I'm pretty sure I could wear a new T-shirt every day of the year and not have to repeat one."

"This one's special," he insisted. He thought he'd be cool and collected, but he wasn't. He thought he knew what she'd say, but he'd learned that if there was one surety in this world it was the fact that there was never anything for sure where Angelina was concerned.

He'd been bringing her T-shirts for months. Funny and cute sayings. This one simply said, *Yes.*

"Yes?" she said, holding it up, clearly puzzled.

Tyler had thought of many ways to do this. He'd mulled it over for weeks. Angelina Tucker wasn't a pop the question at sunset after a romantic date. She wasn't a pop the question on a screen at some big game. He'd even thought about doing it at some party, in front of all her friends and family.

After all his mulling, he'd decided she was exactly the kind of woman who would prefer this. Something unique, but private.

Slowly, he unbuttoned his flannel shirt, his perfectly pressed and tailored flannel shirt, and flashed his T-shirt at Angelina. He didn't need to look down to know it read, *Will you marry me?*

He pointed at her T-shirt and found himself holding his breath, waiting for her to answer. She burst out laughing and said the word he'd been praying for. "Yes. Yes, Tyler Martinez, I will marry you."

She punctuated the sentence with a kiss that told him she meant it. She hadn't needed a T-shirt to prompt her.

"Yes," she repeated and kissed him. "I can't think of anything I want more than taking your name for my own. It means something, your name. Something to be proud of, Tyler. I'm as proud of it as Jace will be some day."

In that instant, Tyler Martinez had everything he wanted in life.

Everything that mattered right here with this woman and the future they were going to build together. The family they'd become.

~~~

Dear Reader,

Thank you for picking up *Suddenly a Father*, the fourth book in my *Hometown Hearts* series. I hope you enjoyed the story. If you did, please leave a review at your favorite online book store. It's the best way to help new readers discover my books. And watch for the fifth book, *Something Borrowed*. It's set in a neighboring town, but it's still got what all small town romances have...heart. There's an upcoming wedding in this hometown...come join in the festivities!

Holly

Hometown Hearts
1. Crib Notes
2. A Special Kind of Different
3. Homecoming
4. Suddenly a Father
A Hometown Hearts Wedding
5. Something Borrowed
6. Something Blue
7. Something Perfect

ABOUT THE AUTHOR

Award-winning author Holly Jacobs has over three million books in print worldwide. The first novel in her Everything But. . . series, *Everything But a Groom*, was named one of 2008's Best Romances by Booklist, and her books have been honored with many other accolades. She lives in Erie, Pennsylvania, with her husband and four children. You can visit her at ***www.HollyJacobs.com***.